This is a work of fiction. Similarities to real people, places, or events are entirely coincidental.

CLAIMING SHANDY RETURN TO WELCOME BOOK 4

First edition. January 18, 2022.

Copyright © 2022 Bonnie Edwards.

ISBN: 978-1989226162

Written by Bonnie Edwards.

I0679672

Table of Contents

This book is dedicated to those who make another attempt, who try again, who don't quit because it's hard. This book is for you.

And to Ted, always.

What readers like you have to say about The Return to Welcome Series:

... I loved the whole family dynamic. I think that was the best part of this. Bonnie Edwards recreates the feel of a small town full of second chances and happy endings. **A heart-warming romance...what more could you want?**

Highland Hussy – 5 STARS Got Fiction? (Book Reviews)

WOW! THIS WAS MORE than I was expecting. Rarely is (this) level of introspection offered. This is my first book by this author, but it won't be my last.

5 STARS Badass Lioness (Book Reviewer)

LOVED IT!! This was a really sweet heartfelt book that you won't want to put down. 5 stars Sissy Mae Hicks (Romance Book Review)

...EMOTIONS IN THIS STORY are poignant and strong... the underlying love they both work so hard to ignore, will not be silenced. **I enjoyed this love story very much.**

5 stars Liza O'Connor – (author and blogger)

Claiming Shandy
Return to Welcome Book 4
By
Bonnie Edwards

At Christmas love returns to Welcome...

Chapter One

December 1 Welcome WA

Justin Camden was no quitter. Never had been and he wasn't about to quit now. But first he had to do battle against the dragons breathing fire in his gut. He'd never been this scared. Not even at fourteen when his dad caught him out driving his mom's car at midnight.

He parked outside the Welcome Bar & Grill and called his buddy, Jake Morrow who was inside with a group of friends. Friends who included Justin's wife, Shandy.

Everything he wanted to accomplish tonight hinged on whatever *BS* line Jake had come up with. "It's me. I'm here. What did you tell her?"

In the background, Justin heard happy people greeting each other over the distant sound of a Christmas song. The season had begun. He climbed out of his car while he heard Jake excuse himself to take the call.

"Bedbugs."

The background noise had receded, but Justin couldn't have heard right. "What?"

"Every hotel in the area's infested. Didn't you know?" Jake said with a smirk in his voice.

"She'll never believe that." He had his hand on the brass door pull. Yanked it toward him.

"I believe she does believe me."

He shook his head. No way. Shandy was the smartest woman he'd ever met and for the past three years, she'd been made of stone. He had to make her crack, but nonsense about bedbugs wouldn't do it. The flame-thrower in his belly belched. Maybe he should turn around and leave.

"Plus, I told Shandy how much Brianna and I are enjoying our honeymoon period," Jake was saying. "She can't force you to stay with us. She has to let you stay at her place. She'll have no choice."

"*Our* place." The home they'd bought together, to raise their family in. "You ass. Bedbugs?" He was inside the vestibule now, looking through the stained-glass partition, searching the restaurant side of the building. "I see the table."

Jake stood a few feet away from the group. "Don't worry, you got this," he said, looking right at him through the multi-colored pane.

"My best and only shot." He ended the call, plastered a smile on his face and made his way through the tables to where Shandy sat beside an empty chair. If this crazy bedbug story worked, he'd have a chance to get her angry. He needed her angry.

If she were angry with him, it was a sign that she still cared. That he could still make her feel something for him.

An angry Shandy was honest, and open. Angry Shandy was not a stone angel, cold and remote, the way she'd been for too long. He needed honest and open or his plan to return to Welcome and be the husband and father he wanted to be would fail.

Justin Camden was no quitter. He doused the flames in his gut.

ON THE RESTAURANT SIDE of the Welcome Bar & Grill, at a long table full of good friends, Shandy Camden was the only one with an empty chair beside her. Maybe next year, she'd have a special someone to join her for these fun evenings. Three years was long enough to be alone. With her son, Josh, getting older, and more understanding, it was time to find a special friend. Or a love.

She eyeballed her friend Jake Morrow, with a jaundiced eye. They'd known each other their whole lives. He was recently married to Brianna, a newer, but close friend. He was a prankster—not as good as he believed—and his bedbug story rang false. It wasn't that Shandy didn't believe bedbugs could infest a hotel. The idea that all the hotels in town were crawling with them at the same time seemed ludicrous. Jake was on his phone a few feet away from the table.

Whatever the reason for this bedbug nonsense, it had nothing to do with her. Acutely aware of the empty seat beside her, she resolved to get to work on dating again. She'd made halfhearted attempts, but nothing short of determined persistence and an open heart would win this battle. For the new year, she promised herself she'd join the Dating Wars and win.

The Welcome Bar & Grill was the most popular place in town for groups to gather for dinner. The other side, the bar side, catered to adults. Men who came in to nurse a beer and hang with buddies, or couples to share a bottle of wine and appetizers. It was also the best place in town to get the juiciest gossip.

Unless you counted the Welcome Bakery. You could catch up on some good drama there sometimes, too. If she started dating, *she'd* be the target of the gossip. Shandy didn't much like being the subject of juicy rumor, so she determined that it should only be the very best kind. The happy kind.

Like, 'did you see the handsome one she was with Saturday night?' kind of juicy. Not the 'he left her flat and heartbroken,' kind of juicy. No. No. *No.* She'd had that when her husband ran off. *Never again.*

Her son, Josh, sat across the table and down a couple of seats beside Dilly, a five-year-old favorite of his, who belonged to Clay and Mercy Foster. Josh liked to help Dilly color and do puzzles.

Smiling at the sweet nature of her son, she studied the drinks menu for something festive to kick off the holiday season. Her last lonely Christmas.

She sighed and believed, without a doubt, that next year's Christmas season would be full of love and the joy of a loving relationship.

She'd just decided on her drink order when her big oaf of an ex-husband landed in the empty chair beside her. *Justin*. She blinked because he wasn't supposed to be here. This wasn't his weekend to visit.

"What are you doing here?" She demanded, out of the side of her mouth so their son wouldn't hear the shock in her voice. *What a pain.*

She didn't allow unscheduled visits and Justin was fully aware. In a world where she'd had no control over anything, she'd put her foot down about a schedule. Until now, he'd complied. Maybe he'd given her short notice a time or two, but she'd been informed. But this unexpected appearance was untenable.

Jerk.

"We talked about you showing up out of the blue, three years ago." She faced him and scowled. Their son couldn't see her expression from where he sat. Besides, he was still focused on Dilly. "You remember," she said smoothly. "That time you ran off and we set up a visitation schedule." *Bitter, much?*

The oaf leaned in. His breath waffled through the hair covering her ear and his aftershave made her blink. The jerk always smelled good, no matter how badly he behaved.

"*You* talked about it," he crooned. "And since this is the first time I've shown up unannounced, you can cut me some slack."

She frowned and seethed inside. He shouldn't be crooning the way he used to. The way that meant he wanted to hit the sheets. He had no right. She pulled back to escape the intent look in his eyes. What game was he playing?

"I went along with you for three years." Justin pulled back, too and kept his voice low and tight. "I miss my son and that beats everything." He waved for the server and when he had the young woman's attention, tapped the menu Shandy had in her hand. To save the server a trip, she passed her menu to the oaf.

"Thanks," he said.

While he read, Shandy glanced around the table. This motley crew of returnees to Welcome and the people who loved them had become her family. Every one of the adults was still and listening, looking back at her with their eyebrows raised in curiosity. She narrowed her gaze at Jake. He knew Justin had planned this stunt and hadn't warned her.

The cockamamie story Jake had concocted about a bedbug infestation at the local hotels made her furious. Jake had set her up somehow. She couldn't connect the dots yet, but she would, and when she did, both the Jays would pay.

Shandy gave her ex such a cold shoulder he should be frozen in his seat. But no, he draped his arm across her shoulders like it belonged there. She shrugged, but he stuck to her, the weight of his arm heavy and warm.

"Buddy, psst, Josh, look who's here for Christmas," he said to the most wonderful boy to grace the planet.

"Wait. What?" Shandy swiveled her face to meet Justin's hazel-eyed stare. "You can't be here for Christmas. Not yet." She kept her terse tone low and deliberate. He'd never returned to Welcome for longer than three days. It was the first of the month, not Christmas Eve. "Tell me this instant what you're up to and I won't poke you in the eye with my salad fork."

"Dad!" Josh wreathed his face in a huge welcoming grin and stabbed his mother in the chest. Right through the heart, just the way his father wanted him to. She sank against the chair back afraid of what came next. Dots were connecting...

Josh looked ecstatic to see the big oaf. Her chest clanged a warning as the joy on her boy's face made her cave, as the oaf knew she would. She was caught in a net, unable to break free. What caring mother could tell her son that his father wasn't welcome at Christmas? Not this mother.

She ground her molars as Josh dashed around the table to greet his father with a big hug. What the heck was the oaf up to now? They'd been divorced for three years, and he'd never pushed back against her policy on unannounced visits. He'd generally abided by her rule to make arrangements in advance for extra visits. She always said yes when he wanted to see their son's school or sports activities. But this? This felt like an ambush.

The drink orders were taken, and Shandy chose a small glass of nice, crisp Riesling. "And a glass of water, please. Hold the ice."

Wine when what she wanted was a barrel full of whiskey to get through this ridiculous nonsense her ex had concocted. She wanted to ignore the delighted chatter of her son who'd wedged himself between her and his father. Thankful she wouldn't get caught up in Justin's eyes again, she focused on the rest of the guests.

Dilly continued coloring a paper mat the server had given her. Her boy was great with younger kids. It gave her a pang that he didn't have younger siblings. Josh wore a buttoned down crisp white shirt and looked every inch the young man he was at ten, while Dilly was in a Christmas-red, velvet dress with snow white lace around the collar. She was adorable with her soft blonde curls going every which way.

Shandy ordered chocolate milk for Josh and Dilly, since her parents, Clay and Mercy were deep in discussion about what Santa would bring for their baby girl, Autumn. Next to them sat Logan and Elle, proud parents to Elle's three children, with another set of twins on the way.

There were various grandparents at the table, too, but it hurt to watch them with their grandchildren because her son would never have that kind of love.

The table was much like her heart; full but with a blank space where she'd love a special someone to be. She wanted a partner and had been hoping one would magically appear for a couple of years, but up to now, no one had. She'd had the odd date here and there, but no one had caught her heart, not in the way she wanted.

There'd been real love once and then he'd turned into a man she didn't recognize and had walked out on their family. And now, he was here saying he was home for Christmas.

It was too much, and she stood, grabbed her purse from where it hung on the back of her chair, and headed to the ladies' room on the bar side. Behind her, she heard a slight commotion, but she didn't look back.

Chapter Two

S handy slammed into the ladies two-stall bathroom on the bar side of the Bar & Grill and stifled a scream by shoving knuckles into her mouth. She walked to the wall across from the door and slammed her back against it.

Feminine voices came from outside the door and Shandy held in tears of frustration as Brianna, Mercy, and Elle barged into the small space.

"You should see your faces," Shandy said with a bark of laughter. "You look like warrior queens leading a charge." She smoothed her fingertips across her cheeks to smear the wet away.

"Did he say he was here for the whole season?" Mercy demanded.

Shandy nodded, but Elle spoke. "That's right," the feistiest woman in Welcome snarled. But her rubbing her belly took the threat out of her tone. Warriors couldn't make efficient war when their bellies were full of babies. Shandy smiled at them, her friends, her support, her warrior queens. They rallied for her as she had done for them.

Brianna was quietly searching Shandy's face. "I wasn't told anything about this. Not that Justin was coming to town and certainly not that he planned to stay for weeks. I'd have warned you."

"Jake's too smart to let you in on anything the Jays planned around me and Josh." The Jays, Jake, and Justin were like brothers. Always had been. As kids nobody saw one without the other and so many people got their names mixed up, they'd been called the Jays since Kindergarten. At least that was the story they told. She hadn't met Justin until high school.

Shandy had fought with Justin over naming Josh, but he'd caught her at a weak moment when her baby had been placed on her tummy. Jake, Justin, Josh...

"And that crap about bedbugs? Really?" Elle again, fuming.

Shandy opened her arms and Elle walked straight into them.

"Ignore me, I'm hormonal," Elle sniffed against her ear. Shandy smoothed her back in comfort. Mercy moved in for a hug too and then Brianna took the other side, and the four women stood a moment, collecting themselves.

"How will you handle a whole Christmas season with your ex hanging around town?" Mercy whispered.

"He's not staying with us," Brianna announced. "And I will padlock the camper out back and throw away the key if Jake thinks he can let him sleep in there."

"Atta girl," Elle said with an inelegant snort.

The hug ended and everyone found a spot to stand comfortably. Elle propped her behind on the counter while Mercy and Brianna leaned against the other walls.

"It's not that I have feelings for Justin," she clarified. "Because he killed those when he left."

Her friends nodded.

"I don't settle, don't back down, and never change direction. When I set a course, I stick to it." There was no going back.

The others murmured agreement. Some men found confidence and determination in women hard to live with, she supposed. At least, Justin had. She couldn't help judging all men by him.

"The big jerk is as stubborn, and bull headed as I am. If he's got a plan to be in Welcome for the month, then he'll be here." She sighed. "I wouldn't put it past him to pitch a tent somewhere. When we married, I expected passionate debate, because of who we were. But never a break-up. Never, ever a divorce." And three years later she still held the vestiges of pain from their joint loss.

"Of course not," Mercy said in a sympathetic tone.

"People don't marry expecting to divorce," Brianna concurred.

Elle raised an eyebrow at Brianna's Pollyanna attitude. "Only the ones looking for a juicy settlement from a rich old guy." She turned her sharp-eyed warrior gaze onto Shandy. "But what will you do about your current problem?"

Shandy had turned three rundown laundromats into a string of six successful ones. "I'll call the hotels to see if they need help laundering their linens in time for their Christmas guests. I'll get to the truth, don't worry."

Mercy cleared her throat. "The problem will be with Josh. How will he feel if you show up his father and prove the bedbug story is a lie?"

The women fell silent for a long moment, but Shandy knew the answer. "I can't make Justin look bad in Josh's eyes." She didn't want to be *that* divorced mother. Up to this point, they'd managed not to tear each other down for their son's sake. Josh was the most important person in the world to them.

Elle nodded. "Since I'm in here anyway, I'll use the facilities. There's no extra room with these babies kicking my bladder all day long." Her comment brought smiles and the mood lightened.

"I'll head back to the table," Shandy said with a salute. "Who knows what the big oaf has promised Josh by now."

When she reclaimed her seat, she doubted she'd been missed. The chatter between father and son continued. Josh loved his dad and Justin was a great father. Had been since day one.

But Justin lived in California, so he missed the day-to-day. He made the trip to see Josh every other weekend without fail. And he showed up for any special events in Josh's life. But he'd never, ever come this early for Christmas.

As a family that no longer lived together, they handled life as best they could by setting aside their bitterness and resentment in order to put Josh first. Generally, they communicated via text or email. She should have been told about this extended Christmas visit.

She shot Jake Morrow a glare sharp enough to stab him through. *Bedbug infestation. Baloney!* At least he had the grace to look guilty when she killed him with her eyes.

Knowing Brianna would put her foot down and refuse Justin her hospitality, the women had turned the Jays prank against them. The thought brought on a smile.

Guilt was written all over Jake's face while Logan Hughes and Clay Foster kept their faces still and their eyes on their half-empty beers. She gave them a pass. They weren't in on this prank.

Josh let out a sudden whoop and ran back around the table to take his seat. A huge smile lit his face and he looked so happy, that when Justin slung his arm across her shoulders again, she didn't have the heart to make him move it.

Or elbow him in the ribs.

"What did you say to him?" she demanded. Inside she simmered with cold anger. This was unfair to Josh. Sure, she and the oaf hid their hurt and disappointment in each other during their brief moments when they were with their son, but this public display of affection went too far. They never showed any in private, so what was Justin up to?

Did the Jays believe she was stupid? But Josh was looking at his parents with wide-open trust and excitement and her heart melted for him. He was only ten. Did he remember a time when they were a family? And happy? Probably not.

Still, she was no pushover.

"Brianna says you're not welcome at their place. And since the hotels are infested with bugs, you can't stay in one of them, either. That's a shame," she said with a too-sweet smile. The heat of him enveloped her and his scent was cozily familiar in a way she hated.

Justin's neck flushed, a sure sign he'd been caught in a lie.

"I'm not welcome at Jake's," he said in a serious undertone. "If you haven't noticed Jake and Brianna are still in the fun honeymoon stage. You remember what that's like." He cleared his throat and leaned in to whisper in her ear. "I couldn't intrude. They're probably getting some all over the house. In the kitchen, the laundry room, the shower..." He trailed away, making her stew over her memories of their early years together.

She flushed hot at the reminders of their younger selves, hot, sweaty, and so in love they couldn't breathe when they were apart. At least, that's how it had been for her. Justin had been her everything, once.

She removed his hand from her shoulder and shrugged him off. "Keep your hands to yourself," she said sharply. She grabbed her phone from her purse and typed a reminder to call the hotels to confirm the infestation. One call to housekeeping would give her what she needed to know.

JUSTIN ALLOWED HIS hand to fall to his lap when Shandy dislodged his arm. His plan would take work and it wouldn't be easy, but this battle had just begun. This micro skirmish was hers, but he'd made his point. His ex-wife may be stubborn but these years apart from her and Josh were over.

She just didn't know it yet.

He was in Welcome for the whole Christmas season. He planned to use this time to find his way back to his family and after the New Year, he'd be home for good. With Josh and Shandy. He hoped.

The plan sounded great in his head, but the reality of Shandy's cold response doused him with doubt. Jake had told him not to push, to take things slow, but now that Justin had decided on a course of action there'd be no stopping until he succeeded.

He'd made the biggest mistake of his life three years ago and he was here to correct it. He wanted his wife and son back and he'd move heaven and earth to get them.

Providing he could soften his wife's attitude toward him.

But Shandy was made of granite, and no one understood that better than he. She was the proverbial hard place when she was angry. And sure, he'd been the rock during their arguments. But he knew better now. He'd be kinder, more patient, and infinitely more understanding.

These three years had nearly broken him, but he'd learned from the experience. Learned and grown.

He hadn't told Jake about his plan to step back into Shandy's life. That's what this month was about: talking with her, being with her, eating meals with her, spending time alone with her. This holiday season would be about wooing Shandy.

Claiming Shandy.

Chapter Three

Justin was determined that come the New Year, he, Shandy, and Josh would be a family again. It was everything Justin wanted, and having his father home again would be best for Josh.

For now, he'd be content to sit beside the only woman for him and enjoy the company of good, old friends.

It was different, but good to see Jake here with Brianna since his buddy had spent the last decade pushing everyone away. But that had changed through the summer and Justin couldn't be happier for his best friend. He couldn't help being a bit envious. Jake and Brianna had rekindled their feelings after a decade apart.

Surely, he and Shandy could do the same after only three. Plus, they had Josh to think of. If a great kid like him couldn't help cement his parents, then there was no hope.

Despite all that had happened between him and Shandy, Justin *did* have hope. He'd been an ass, a jerk, a fool. Shandy had been granite in her stubbornness. He'd seen a side of her he couldn't believe.

The server had returned to take their food orders. As he considered the menu, he became aware of the scent of flowers whenever Shandy moved. He drank it in and remembered when he had the right to nuzzle her hair and nibble her earlobe and everything had been right between them.

Before.

Voices rose around him as the friendly group moved on from the surprise of his arrival. Shandy's friends had followed her to the ladies room in that mysterious way of women. When they returned, they'd passed him smirking glances. Clearly, his wife had friends at her back.

Good. She'd dedicated her life to Josh when he was young, and she'd fallen out of touch with a lot of her female friends.

Elle was one to watch though. The looks she was giving him were deadly. Brianna looked concerned in her quiet way and Mercy looked half amused. But every one of them had Shandy's back and he'd have to step carefully around them.

He'd believed the only person he had to convince about his reversal of attitude, was his ex, but these friends would watch him, too. And they'd report whatever they noticed to Shandy. He'd have to be extra careful about what he said to Jake because of Brianna.

Glancing from man to man around the table, he realized no single men had joined the group. Good. No one else was here for Shandy. He didn't expect any resistance from the women's husbands.

Clay Foster was Elle's brother and married to Mercy. Back in the day he was a different guy. The Clay here held a baby in the crook of his arm and deftly managed to eat appetizers one-handed, without dropping anything on the baby's lily-white blanket. The Clay Justin recalled from high school had been a powder keg waiting to go off. He'd been dark and moody and had had all the girls he wanted. Clearly, these days, he was dedicated to his wife and children.

Logan Hughes, on the other hand, was the same as Justin remembered. He'd been known as a nice guy, never rocked the boat and from all accounts, he was still as helpful as ever. The news that he'd married Elle Foster, the snarkiest girl in high school and Clay's sister, surprised Justin, but Jake said they were poster children for happy marriage. *Opposites really do attract.*

The only person to give Justin pause was Josh. His son had to be protected from having expectations around his plan. He'd be careful not to get the boy's hopes up. If Josh mentioned the family reuniting, Shandy would put a stop to things, and it would take much longer to convince her to take him back.

As tempting as it was to include Josh in his plan to return to his marriage, Justin had to tread carefully. Hurting Josh couldn't happen.

Wouldn't happen.

Justin would play things cool and be reasonable without tipping his hand too soon.

Logan asked him a question about life in California. He smiled and told him the truth.

"It's sunnier than here, but I find it lonely without Josh. Two weeks in the summer with him doesn't cut it." His promotions at the winery had come as promised and he'd done better than he'd hoped. But things were about to get more interesting than he could have anticipated. He couldn't share anything with anyone yet, though.

Logan flashed a look at Shandy, who stiffened in response to Justin's comment. "Yeah, I can see how that would be tough," Logan said. "How's work?"

The dreaded question. He gave a cool smile. "It's good. The promotion when I changed jobs turned into two more. I'm set." Beside him, Shandy made a *hmph* sound meant for his ears only.

She assumed he was happy with how his life was going. But, on the weekends he wasn't here with Josh, he was working. He had no time to himself, no time for a life and he hated it. The thing that gnawed the worst was that Shandy had told him this would happen. He'd fall into a workaholic routine and lose out. But he was only working this hard because he had nothing outside of work. He didn't date or do anything away from the office.

The only thing that had kept him from completely disappearing into his career was having Josh. And now, the hope that Shandy might take him back. God, he'd been such a stupid, callous, ambitious fool. But ambition had brought him back home and he'd never have to leave Welcome again.

"Hey, Babe, you're not eating," he said next to her ear. "The appetizers are great." He popped a deep-fried crab ball into his mouth and chewed.

"I'm fine," she muttered and reached for her glass of wine. "Just dandy. And don't call me Babe."

"I don't think you are fine, though," he said. "Sorry about the old name, it slipped out." He'd been caught up in her scent and having her this near disconcerted him. For three years, they'd stayed well apart, physically. Usually, no closer than speaking distance. He drew in a deep breath, wishing he could hold her scent in his nose for the rest of the night. It calmed him.

She turned away from him, clearly disgusted with his lame excuse. He had to be more careful. To Josh he said, "Isn't your holiday talent show at school this week?"

Josh looked up with a happy, expectant grin. "Yeah, it's Thursday night."

"Good. I'll be there." He let the comment sit in the air while Josh cheered. His little friend Dilly cheered too.

"WHAT GAME ARE YOU PLAYING?" Shandy asked Justin. "Normally you'd come for whatever Josh is doing and head home early the next morning." He left on time because he'd never miss a day of work. No. Not Justin.

"This is not a game," her ex said in a deep, determined tone. "I'm here and I'm staying."

"But by Thursday you'll be bored. Antsy to get back to work. Meanwhile, Josh will look forward to you being here for the school talent show. You and I know you'll be back at work by then." He was always working. Work was his whole life.

He'd made that plenty clear three years ago when he'd walked out.

The long table full of friends paused in their conversation and then as if by unspoken agreement, took a drink. Some had wine, some had beer, while the nursing or pregnant mothers enjoyed virgin cocktails.

The oaf attempted to look ingenuous. She snorted in derision.

"I'm here for the whole month, four whole weeks." Justin replied, lifting one corner of his mouth. A sure sign he was trying to get away with something. "All the way to the New Year."

Could he say it any more ways? "Why? Why are you here? What reason do you have for such a long visit?" If he could talk in triples, so could she. She held her breath, willing the three-year-old child in her head to shut up. Justin had pulled her right back to the type of sniping they'd used when hell had rained fire on their marriage.

He went on blandly when he saw her stony expression. "I have vacation days I have to use or lose. I'm spending the time here."

"Where will you stay?"

"In the house, since I can't stay with Jake and the hotels are in a sorry state."

She couldn't have heard right.

She wanted to splutter and howl and spit like a fury, but with Josh watching, she controlled her temper. "You don't think checking with me first would have been a good idea?"

"No. Actually, I didn't think you'd mind." He widened his eyes like an innocent.

Liar. "I see." He'd never cared to take vacation time before. "Why now?"

"Is it terrible to want a whole Christmas season with my son?"

Christmas. Hah! Shandy slid her eyelids down to cover her reaction. *Get a grip. You can't tear him into here.*

"It's terrible to put us through this again," she whispered with her eyes still closed. He understood clearly what "this" was. Tiptoeing around Josh, pretending they were friendly, when they were anything but. *And at Christmas!* The lie seemed doubly wrong.

She popped open her eyes in time to see that she'd scored with that jab. Justin's expression filled with doubt then rallied.

"Let me stay with you for a few days," he urged. "We'll keep busy with all the Christmas activities in town. We'll do everything we did with Josh when he was little. Time's going too fast and I'm missing out on his life. As it is, I'll never get back the three years I've been away."

The oaf wasn't missing anything. He was in Welcome a lot. Chewing her lip, she considered a few days spent with Justin in the house. He was a handy guy with tools, and she had repairs to see to. "When he's in school, you'll help me out. I have a lot for you to do around the house and in some of the laundromats." She glared at him. "If I have to tolerate you, then I need to get something for my trouble."

"I'm your guy," Justin said with the smile that had stolen her heart years ago. Damn the man.

"Starting with putting up my outdoor light display tomorrow." She wouldn't help. Absolutely not.

"Hey, Buddy. Want to help me string the lights on the house? We'll start in the morning."

"Sure!" Josh said, halfway to a yell.

"Might take the whole day."

"That's okay, Dad. It'll be fun."

She was doomed.

Two hours later, back at her place, Shandy's trepidation rose as she kissed her boy goodnight. "Have a good night. I love you, Josh."

"Are you okay?" his sleepy voice was aimed at the pillow, but she heard his concern. At ten, he didn't often consider her feelings, or believe she had them, but there were flashes of the caring man he would become someday. Her heart filled.

"I'm fine. Everything will be okay," she promised as she brushed the top of his head with her lips. *If his dad didn't try to get him to move to California, they'd be fine.*

She wasn't sure what had prompted this sudden prolonged visit, but it was more than Justin was letting on. He waited out in the hall for his turn to say goodnight. She left her son's room, leaving the door open so she could eavesdrop, feeling no guilt.

A minute later, Justin joined her in the hall. He hadn't said anything but goodnight.

She gently closed the bedroom door and turned briskly toward the head of the stairs. "The linen and a spare pillow are in the closet here." She pointed to a narrow door, as if he'd forgotten the layout of the house. Maybe he had. Maybe he'd gone to California and put everything they'd done together into a dusty basement in his mind.

They'd been full of joy and anticipation of a shiny future when they'd chosen this house before Josh was born. But three years ago when things had fallen apart, they'd backed out of the sale without being sued. So, the house, *their home,* was still hers.

With a sigh, she saw that she was the one who needed to shove her memories away.

"No need, I brought an air mattress and everything else I'll need," he was saying. "I'll park myself in the den. I noticed the guestroom is now a workout studio."

"The den will be fine." She led the way to the main floor and walked into her den. Justin had already put a box containing the air mattress and a large bag full of linen on the floor. "I'll just be a moment," she muttered, and sat behind her desk. Methodically, she collected every scrap of paper, mostly bills and receipts, and locked them in a drawer in the file cabinet in the corner. Next, she closed and unplugged her laptop. She held it as she stepped to the door, afraid of the silence as Justin watched her with amused eyes.

"I'm not here to snoop into your affairs."

She spun to him. "Then, why are you here? Is it to take Josh away to live with you?" she demanded, sounding strident. Scared of his answer, she held her breath.

His startled look seemed genuine, and her heart eased a fraction. "Of course not," he replied with some heat. "I'd never disrupt your lives that way. What kind of ogre do you think I am?"

"How would I know? I never thought you'd leave me—*us*—either, but you did." Tears threatened and she dashed from the room before he could see them. That would be humiliating, and she'd been humiliated enough for one lifetime.

She hated that she still cared what Justin thought of her. She especially hated that she wondered if he remembered anything of the love they'd shared.

Whatever happened over these next few days, she had to keep a tight rein on her emotions. To do that, she'd have to harden her heart. She heard movement behind her and then his voice in the softly lit hall.

"We need to talk," Justin said, sounding gentle, but she ignored him. They'd done their talking and yelling three years ago. She'd needed to stay in Welcome and he'd wanted to leave. And that's what happened.

Chapter Four

The next morning, Shandy held the ladder while Justin clipped lights onto the gutters on the front porch. She wasn't even tempted to shake the ladder, she told herself with some pride.

Josh had been given the job of untangling another string of lights and he was working quietly beside her. The lights had been tested and every bulb had lit up. "After this," she said to him, "we'll drape lights across the bushes, and we're done."

"Dad said we could go to Welcome Hardware and get some blow up people, like a Santa and Mrs. Claus."

This was the first she'd heard of the plan to get inflatables. She didn't need more decorations because she had enough to handle on her own. Next year, Justin wouldn't be here to hang the lights from the gutters, and she'd have to do it. He'd brought the extra strings with him. He'd planned it all along. Until now, she and Josh had been content to keep the decorations simple and lower to the ground.

She'd learned to do a lot of things around the house without her husband's help. She glared up at her ex but directed her words to her son. "You can go with your dad. I'll trust you to pick out the best ones."

No way did she want to spend more time than necessary with Justin. When they'd left the Bar & Grill last night, she'd been determined to give him the too-short sofa to sleep on, but no, he'd arrived with a queen-sized air mattress, pillow, and linen that he'd set up in her den. Now, not only was he in her face; he was comfortable to boot. *Aggravating man!*

He'd deliberately put her in an untenable position. She couldn't kick him out, couldn't yell at him for showing up uninvited because of Josh.

Because it was Christmas.

This forced and phony friendliness would be the end of her. *Hm.* Maybe that was his plan from the start; to wear her down until she faded away to nothing. Stress-induced death by ex-husband contact. They could end up on one of those murder-porn news shows. With a cause of death like ex-husband exposure, they'd make the big time.

Dark suspicion rose. He'd said he wouldn't mess up their lives, but what other reason could there be for him to be here?

She'd have to ask, but first she needed to calm down. She hadn't forgotten his comment about having Josh for two weeks in the summer not being enough. Maybe that's what this was about. Maybe he wanted to negotiate for more time with Josh at his place.

Justin had also said they needed to talk, but she'd been too upset to go back to the den to discuss his real plans. Her frustration had taken an opportunity away from her. Keeping her head in the sand was a bad idea. She needed to control her emotions around the oaf and be more clear-headed.

"I have a date for lunch, so you two go to the hardware store without me," she blurted. The air suddenly turned chill around them. "I'll be back in time for supper." She flashed the oaf a look from under her beetled browns. "Justin, you can handle that, right?"

The ladder jiggled as he climbed down. From three rungs up, he jumped to the ground with a soft thud, forcing her to step back. Justin was only a couple of inches taller than her five feet eight inches, but he was broad, making her feel swamped by his physicality.

"A date?" he asked. He narrowed his eyes as he studied her.

"Yes," she said, letting her face go slack. It was only a lunch date with Brianna, but still, she refused to cancel. She'd come to depend on her circle of friends to keep her grounded and given her messy holiday season this year, she needed grounding. "Then I'm stopping in to see my mother."

Something like sympathy crossed his gaze. But she must be mistaken. Justin had never shown one iota of caring or understanding. "She's the same? No change?"

Shandy shook her head. "I'd have told you."

"Do you want me to go with you?"

She frowned at his offer. "Of course not." She turned and stalked into the house. The nerve of him, pretending he cared.

"AND THEN HE ASKED IF he could come with me to see her. I'm angry enough to spit. He's never cared about her. About my responsibility." Shandy's voice sounded bitter, like it belonged to someone else, and she hated the sour, whiny flavor of it on her tongue. "Sorry, old baggage. But he really hits my buttons sometimes. The old anger and disappointment shouldn't come up anymore, but his moving in and forcing me to welcome him grates my last nerve."

"I get that," Brianna said softly as they strolled the riverside walkway together. They'd brought along takeout cappuccinos after their lunch at the Welcome Bakery. The air was crisp today, the sun playing peek-a-boo through some high cloud cover. All in all, a nice day for early December. "But he's here for Josh," her friend added.

Brianna was right. Justin was always available to Josh. She should feel lucky that her ex had never shirked on his responsibility to their boy. Lucky and happy that Josh didn't feel neglected, but it was a pain to admit the oaf was a good father.

She didn't want to give Justin credit for anything. It interfered with her disappointment and anger and both those emotions were comfortable now and she wore them like a cloak. "You're quiet and calming, Brianna. It's a knack you have, and I need it now."

Her friend patted her shoulder. "I'm here for you."

"After the summer you had I'm surprised you're not a ball of anxiety and stress." She chuckled. "But maybe I'm projecting my own feelings onto you." Brianna and Jake had suffered through a stalking turned violent. By the end, lives had been at stake.

Brianna nodded. "I'm glad they found Theda's camper van in the woods and the notes she left behind, but once she died, I worked hard to regain my equilibrium. I didn't want her destroying that. Or coming between Jake and me ever again."

"The counselling helped I assume?" Shandy, Mercy, Elle, and Brianna and her mom had witnessed a horrible scene that afternoon and the peace of Welcome had been shaken to its foundations.

"Talking to a professional helped a lot," her friend admitted. "If you want the name of my counsellor, I'll give it to you."

"I'll give that serious consideration. Thank you. I'm sure Justin was helpful to Jake during that time." The events with the stalker had escalated quickly, leaving the town in an uproar.

"Jake is grateful he had Justin to bounce things off. Justin knew there were problems with Theda early, but Jake, being Jake, couldn't wrap his head around a woman exhibiting signs of being an abuser." Brianna smiled softly.

"But that's in the past and we're faced with a whole new thing now," Brianna went on. "Your ex-husband has come home to roost." And gentle Brianna had firmly turned the conversation to the here and now and put the past where it belonged.

"What will I do about the big oaf being in my house? He and Josh are close, and I'd be the bad guy if I put my foot down and kicked Jake out. He brought an inflatable mattress and his own linen, so he'd be comfortable. He's entrenching himself in my home."

"Rock and a hard place," Brianna said with a nod of understanding. "It's Christmas and that brings expectations of family being together."

"Every other year, he's stayed with Jake over the holiday. And he only visited for a couple of nights. He was normally gone by the twenty-seventh to see his parents in San Diego for New Year's Eve."

Shandy spent New Year's Eve alone ever since her marriage fell apart. She'd see her mom and then take Josh out to dinner and a movie. She'd come home to watch the ball drop in Times Square. Big doings at her place every year. *Whoop-de-doo.*

Last time, she'd let New York's time zone work for midnight, and she'd been in bed when the new year came to Welcome. *Nine p.m.* She sighed.

Pathetic. She was living like a woman twenty years her senior. Maybe thirty years. She sighed again, long, and hard, as her lonely future stretched before her.

"It's time I started swiping right," she said. "I'd hoped to find someone in Welcome, but in three years I haven't managed more than a date or two with the same man." She'd had a fling while away on vacation once, but that was it. All fun and no strings.

"People here envision you with Justin and only him. A lot of eligible men left town after college and haven't returned. Don't get me wrong, Welcome's a great place to raise children, but it's also a wonderful town to get out of, too. I enjoyed my years away and without my mom's knee surgery, I'm not sure I'd have come back."

"But look at you now. You're writing a novel, and have a future with Jake, you're working at your own pace with your virtual assistant business, too. You've got it all."

Brianna smiled and nodded. "Nice try deflecting. This conversation is avoiding your problem. What to do about Justin?" Brianna tapped her index finger against her chin.

"I'll have to suck it up and let him stay. He's pulled the prank of a lifetime here, but I can't let him get to me."

"What if you turned the tables?"

"How?"

"What if you showed him what he's missing and can never have again?"

Shandy sipped her cappuccino, savoring the rich, mellow flavor. "I'm not sure what you mean..." she trailed off as visions of seduction danced in her head. She couldn't, could she?

"If your robe happened to slip down your shoulder, or fall open, he'd notice, right?"

"Riiight." Shandy nodded. "And if he made a move, I could shut him down so hard he suffers."

"How long could a man withstand that kind of pressure?"

"Not long. I could drive him out of the house in two or three days." She'd have to be careful not to let Josh see any of her come-hither looks or flirting. The last thing she wanted was to get her son's hopes up for a reunion.

She and Justin had been white-hot for each other once. If she could tap into those memories, Justin would drool. All she'd have to do to drive him out is remind him of what had torn them apart: his blind ambition and drive to get out of Welcome in the first place.

"I'm calling this operation, *Seducing Justin*. What do you think?"

"It might work," Brianna said with a slight frown gathering between her brows. "But won't you seduce yourself at the same time?"

"Not a chance. Not when Justin abandoned me when I needed him most. I'll keep that front and center in my mind," she said coldly. "If I'd known he could be this sneaky and pigheaded I would never have married him in the first place."

She'd have married someone else and had the real life she'd wanted. In Welcome.

IN ROOM 108 OF THE Welcome Nursing Home, Shandy leaned over the bed and kissed her mother's forehead. "Hi, Mom, it's Shandy.

I love you and miss you." She blinked back tears. They'd never helped, not here, with her mom or with Justin.

"The nurse told me you had a restless night. I'm sorry about that. I have those sometimes, too." She settled into her chair beside the bed and slipped her hand to cover her mom's. "But you already know that because we've talked about them before.

"Aside from me worrying about the regular stuff single mothers fret about, I have a new problem. Justin's back."

Brenda Armstrong's lips moved as if she heard and understood the strain her ex-son-in-law's return had brought. "Not permanently, of course, but he's here for the Christmas season because he has some time off work." She chuckled. "Yes, I know what you're thinking. Justin never takes time off. And it's only December second. Surely, he doesn't mean to stay for the whole month."

Shandy tucked her mom's hand back under the sheet. She'd been bathed and her hair looked clean and shiny. Brenda would be shocked to know how lovely her gray hair was. Soft waves of baby fine hair wisped about her shoulders and there were still strands of gold and brown threaded through the gray. It was so pretty that Shandy considered letting hers go gray when the time came.

"I don't want you to get your hopes up. Justin's only here to spend time with Josh, not with me. On Thursday we'll go to the school's winter talent show. Josh is doing some magic tricks. I gave him that kit last summer, remember?"

A slight grimace passed across Brenda's face and Shandy sighed. These tiny signs meant nothing. Brenda was comfortable, but non-responsive to her voice. It was a matter of time before her mother failed completely and Shandy would be without her.

These visits had become easier as she'd accepted the inevitable. She used to bring Josh with her for each visit, back when she hoped hearing him might help her mom come back to them. But nothing had helped, and Josh had become distant and sad on those visiting days.

Her parents had loved being grandparents and had been very close to Josh.

Shandy had felt orphaned by the car accident that had taken her father and left her mother in this state. Josh lost two people he'd always counted on at once. And then, to make matters worse, his father had left. Nothing would get her past that betrayal. She held onto her anger and grief like a weighted blanket. It was comfortable to hold those emotions close and to use them as a barrier against Justin.

"Sometimes I still can't believe how quickly life can change. But if it can change for the worse in the blink of an eye, it can also change for the better, too. Dad used to say that. I'd be disappointed by something at school, and he'd say I should wait for the good stuff because it was right around the corner." Her lips lifted at the memory. But as much as she loved what her dad used to say, there was no way anything good would come from Justin returning to Welcome.

Chapter Five

By the next morning, as she cracked eggs into a pan, Shandy reconsidered her foolish decision to pretend to seduce her husband. Justin was a man like any other. The faintest hope of sex would keep him here, not drive him away.

Add to that, she'd never been able to resist Justin's dark auburn hair and green eyes. His inherent appeal had been like a drug in their early days together. He'd always been attractive to her. She'd fallen hard for him that first awkward night they'd met.

She'd been a bit tipsy and a lot rebellious and had needed a ride home from the lake where a bunch of teens had celebrated the end of high school.

Unfortunately, one look at Justin Camden had made her curse her stupidity for having given her virginity to a boy who had a reputation for not looking twice at the same girl. Teenage hormones and beer made for poor decisions. Even today, she sighed with regret, though she'd forgiven the foolishness of her youth. Hers and the bad boy's.

She'd met Justin twenty minutes too late.

Stirring the pan full of scrambled eggs, she heard the coffee carafe slide out of its cradle on the kitchen island behind her. The oaf was up. She didn't look over her shoulder to greet him.

"Good morning," Justin's early-morning-rough voice came to her and for a millisecond she flashed on the days when they'd been happy. She'd have turned to him with a smile, walk over for a kiss, and then load his plate for him.

Not today.

Never again.

"Hi, Dad," Josh said from where he sat at the kitchen table. "Mom's making eggs, want some?"

"Nothing would be sweeter, Buddy."

She heard him sip his coffee. Too bad she'd only made enough eggs for two, she thought with a smirk. Josh ate like an adult now.

Shandy plated a scoop of eggs for Josh and the rest for herself, shut off the gas burner and turned with both plates in hand. "You'll have to make your own," she said to the jerk taking up too much room in her kitchen.

She gave him a wide berth as she wound around the island to the table to sit with her son.

"Sure thing," the big oaf said with a grin. "I'll drive you to school, Josh."

"No, I'll take him," she interjected, cutting off her son's agreement before it was born. "Just because you're here, doesn't mean we change our routine." She forked up some eggs quickly. The sooner she finished, the faster she'd be away from the oaf.

"I don't want to mess with your routine." Justin opened the fridge and rummaged. It took all she had not to ask what he was looking for, but she refused to make his forced visit more comfortable. The man was perfectly capable of fending for himself.

After all, he'd had three years to learn to cook his breakfast and do his laundry. And he'd taken the last of the coffee without offering to make more. Great, now she had indigestion. She slid her plate of half-eaten eggs to the side.

"Did you see the blow-up people we got?" Josh asked around a mouthful of toast.

"I did. If you like them, then I do, too," she said. She refrained from pointing out that he'd talked with his mouth full. There was only so much she could handle, and her focus was on making Justin feel unwelcome.

When she'd come home after seeing her mother, she seen the inflatables. On the lawn, Justin and Josh had arranged a Santa and Mrs. Claus. They stood together holding hands and waving to passersby, while three of their elves gamboled next to them in a pile of fluffy white plastic that was supposed to look like snow. When they weren't filled with air, they looked like flat, large, colorful flags on the lawn.

She wondered if there was some message in the happy looking group but shut down the idea before it took her down a wrong path. Sending subliminal messages was too sophisticated for Justin. He wasn't a man who hinted. No. He took what he wanted.

Just like he'd taken his exit when it suited him to leave his family.

JUSTIN SHOULDN'T HAVE taken Jake's advice to get the happy Claus couple and happier looking elves. It was stupid to assume Shandy would fall for such a broad hint. But Jake had seemed convinced that she'd get the message that he wanted his family back.

No, that wasn't right. *They* hadn't been the ones to leave. He was the one who moved to California.

And now he was the one who wanted to return to them and to Welcome. Damn, he had a lot to make up for. He slanted Shandy a glance as he realized he'd taken the last of the coffee.

She was so pretty in the morning. Fresh and happy. Before, she'd have been wearing one of his old tees and a pair of sleeping shorts while making breakfast.

Today, she was fully covered in wooly socks, jeans, and a long-sleeved baggy sweater that hid all her curves.

Still, he remembered what was under the camouflage. Desire tore through him. It had been too long since he'd held her. Made love to her. He'd danced in a bar with a woman once or twice since leaving

Welcome, making sure she was Shandy's height and approximate size. He'd close his eyes and pretend. Pitiful and pathetic.

She slid her plate of eggs to the side, looking disgusted with them. She propped her chin on her hand, making her lips pout. Once, he'd have walked over and kissed the pout away. She'd have smiled and kissed him back.

This morning, she wouldn't look him in the eye. He set the carton of eggs on the counter and blew out a breath, trying to ease his frustration. But his attempt to soften her had just begun and he had a whole month to keep trying.

"I'll make us more coffee," he offered, if only to spend a few minutes sipping and enjoying a cup with her.

"Don't bother, I have things to do." His wife rose from the table, tossed him a glare, and headed toward the stairs in the hall. He listened as she thundered up and then stomped across the floor overhead.

Josh's face was raised toward the ceiling, too. "She's mad about something, but I can't tell if it's me or you," he said with the logic of a ten-year-old.

"I can pretty much guarantee it's me," Justin replied. "It's always me."

"Why are you here?" Josh asked.

Justin's brain stuttered to a stall at the simple question. He couldn't give his son the real reason. Not yet. Getting the boy's hopes up would be the worst thing a dad could do. Even he knew that, and he wasn't much of a father.

"I've missed a lot of stuff with you this year," he fudged. "I want to make up for it now. And I've got a bunch of vacation days left this year that I want to spend with you."

"Okay," but Josh looked unconvinced. Still, he went back to smearing jam on his last piece of toast, so Justin let it ride. Except...

"It's okay that I'm here, right? There's no reason I shouldn't be?" *Will my being here interfere because your mom's dating some guy?* But he didn't have the guts to ask that.

"Yeah, it's okay. I'm not used to it anymore, that's all." Josh shrugged and finished chugging his glass of milk.

"Let me know if me being around starts to bug you."

"Sure. But you should say that to Mom, too." He collected his dirty dishes, then added his mom's plate to his collection.

"I'll give it due consideration." *Not going to happen.* "I'll pick you up after school if you want. Maybe we can hit the mall in Bellingham and find a gift for your mom for Christmas."

"Mom might not like you picking me up. Let me tell her on the way to school."

Smart boy.

"I've got twenty-five dollars to spend." Josh looked proud of his financial status. "I get allowance for helping out."

"Great." He cracked a couple of eggs into the pan to fry. "Got any ideas for a gift?"

"She wants some smelly stuff, like lotion and soap. She likes to smell like flowers." He carried his empty dishes to the dishwasher. "I looked at the bottles she uses."

"Smelly stuff it is. I'm sure I remember her favorite brand, but if that's changed, tell me. And you shouldn't have to spend all your money, either." His wife had simple tastes and her scent could be found in any pharmacy. Once she found something she liked, she stuck with it.

Except for him.

Chapter Six

D*ecember 5 - Wednesday*

"I have an emergency at one of my Bellingham locations," Shandy told Justin over the phone. He was with Jake doing whatever grown friends did while Josh was at school. Jake was a paramedic, so he had shifts. Today, he was off, and the Jays had planned a day together. "I have to be there for the evening," she explained. "I'll close up at ten."

"You don't have anyone else?" His tone was brusque, and she didn't care for it.

"Most of my staff are single mothers and they have emergencies, just like I do occasionally, because I'm a single mother too. Or have you forgotten?" she sniped.

"I don't like you being there alone at night," he muttered, sound contrite.

She relented because the dig she'd given him had been satisfying. "I have other on-call staff members, but they're already covering shifts in other locations." She had a couple of reliable university students to call on who were happy to be paid to sit at the counter and study until closing time.

"What's going on? Seems like a lot of emergencies at once."

"There's a bug going around, and kids are home from school. They need their moms and if mom has no backup, they stay home from work. But apparently this thing doesn't last long. Only a day or two." She hoped Josh didn't catch it, but at least his father was around to help.

"When will you be home?" Justin pulled her back from her concerns.

"Why? Do you have plans?" She stiffened. *Did he have a date?* He'd been visiting here a few days and with Josh in school, he'd had enough free time to meet someone.

"Of course not. I'll get Josh from school, give him supper, and have something ready for you when you get home. I wish I could be in two places at once. I don't like that you're alone in there at closing time."

Relieved he was available to help with Josh, she softened her tone and eased the stiffness in her back. "Sometimes, it comes down to me being there or the shop closing early, which makes everything worse. Clothes aren't pressed, orders back up. If someone's left the shop with clothes in a washer or dryer, they can't get back in to get them until the next day. I can't mess up customers that way. It's not right. And I'd get a lot of bad word of mouth." She needed to be there. "What's with all the questions?"

"I don't mean anything by them. I'm curious. We haven't talked much this week."

"You're right, we haven't." That was on her. She'd walked away from him whenever he'd wanted small talk. Maybe it was time to let him see how life had evolved for her since he'd left. "It's not easy being a single parent. There are lots of problems and stresses around kids." She sighed. "And if you're skating the edge of living broke, it's much harder than it is for me. I have a home and money. And an ex-husband who visits his son. Some of my employees aren't in my position."

The silence from his end was telling. She'd gotten through to him on some level.

Her dad had left her three rundown locations, and she'd added services, updated machines, and increased staff in the time since he'd died. Wash'n'Suds was a going concern with three more new locations, and she was proud of how far the business had come. It was hectic sometimes and other times, things ran smoothly. But the school year was full of challenges because of all the extracurricular activities which meant missed school bus rides. Every fall child illness spread like wildfire. Lots of after school caregivers like grandparents fell like dominoes to colds brought home by their grandchildren.

"What do you do about Josh when I'm not here?"

"I have a daycare provider, Candace Markham, who keeps him for me. He walks to her place after school and hangs with her. He has dinner there and then they watch movies together until I get home." Candace enjoyed his company and she even helped with homework.

"I remember Candace. Her mom owns the Welcome Bakery."

"Right."

"Good," he said vaguely, but she was too rushed to wonder what it was he approved of: that Candace was her sitter or that her mom was the best baker in town.

LATER THAT EVENING, Justin waited by the front door for Shandy's car to pull into the driveway. Stupid to feel anxious, but she was later than she said she'd be. Anything could have happened to a lone woman closing a shop at ten p.m. in a strip mall. Lights from a vehicle appeared in the distance and he stepped back from the door to watch from the shadows in the living room.

Thank you, God. She was home, safe and sound. Shandy climbed out of her car, wearing her exhaustion in the slump of her shoulders. Her usual bounce was gone, worn down by hours behind a counter.

He hotfooted it into the kitchen and hit the warm-up button on the microwave. He didn't want to make her wait long for the food he had for her.

She walked in, hung her coat up in the hall closet and wandered into the kitchen, looking tired. Still, she smiled. "Do I smell food?"

She wore a happy red Christmas sweater with a striped candy cane on the front. Her jeans were black and slimming. Dust clung to her clothes.

"I ordered Thai for you. Figured you'd need something to eat. I ordered it at ten so it's still fresh, just a bit cool." The timer chimed and he opened the door of the microwave oven. "Did a lint trap explode on you?"

"Something like that. I was folding a lot of flannel. Sheets, nightshirts, and robes. It was a blizzard of fluff." She walked up behind him and slipped her fingers to his shoulder as she drew a deep inhale through her nose. "Smells like heaven."

He looked at her from the corner of his eyes, startling her as she realized she'd touched him. Her hand fell away as if she'd been scalded.

She shifted back, out of touching range. As she moved, he scented her flowery fragrance. He was sure that Josh had been right about her favorite.

He lifted the container out of the oven. "There's a plate and cutlery on the counter."

"Great, thanks. I'll go wash up." She turned and left for the half bath in the hall. Water ran as he set her food on the counter and grabbed a can of ginger ale out of the fridge. He put the kettle on in case she wanted a hot drink.

"How did it go?" he asked as she settled onto the stool across the island.

"Fine," she said, sounding weary. "I'm glad we offer fluff and fold services until I have to do it. How were things here?"

"Josh and I ordered pizza and played video games. Bedtime was a breeze. He's a great kid, and I have you to thank." He'd told her the other day what a big help he was tidying up the kitchen after breakfast. Justin approved of Josh earning an allowance.

Shandy's hand stilled on her fork where it lay beside her plate. She blinked and looked at him. "You're welcome. But you've been here, too. Despite living far away, you never miss your weekend with him." Her blue-eyed gaze was fatigued, serious, and honest. Then it dropped to her food, and they lost the connection.

Of course, he put his son before anything else, he always had. But still, it pleased him that she'd noticed and appreciated it. He watched for a moment while she ate. After the second bite she moaned lightly in pleasure.

"Delicious," she mumbled around her mouthful.

Viscerally, he remembered her moans and how much he loved to bring them on. He was the biggest idiot on the planet for walking away. And then, stupidly, he'd accepted the divorce. He should have fought for her and for Josh. He'd been a world class fool.

He'd do anything to change the past and his lousy decisions. His bullheadedness. The realization nearly did him in. He turned away to hide the yearning that must be in his eyes. Things would be different now, though. He'd get exactly what he'd come back to Welcome for.

"I have six locations now," she said. The blithe comment pulled him around to face her. "They keep me busy."

"I had no idea you'd expanded to that degree." He'd been made aware that she'd opened her fourth because she'd told him she wouldn't need his support money to live on. They'd agreed it would go into his college fund. "Josh didn't say anything about new stores."

She shrugged and took another forkful of rice. "After four, it became no big deal, I guess. They mean more to me than to anyone else."

"And I've never asked for updates," he said quietly. "Congratulations. That's impressive. You're impressive." He leaned against the counter, searched her gaze. "You handle this house, our son, and a growing business."

She moved her shoulders as if shifting a weight. Maybe she didn't feel as successful as she actually was. Being tired could rob a person of a sense of accomplishment. "The three locations my dad left me were old and needed updating." She glanced at him as she ate another forkful. "That was a major challenge. The machines needed overhauling, not duct tape fixes. But once I got the fourth location, a place I picked myself, things clicked. I found I enjoyed looking for locations, hiring the right people and setting things up." She surprised him by reaching for his glass of ginger ale and taking a sip. He got her a can and a glass of her own.

"You never told me you needed help."

She shook her head and poured her drink. "Because I didn't need help. I needed to keep busy and focused on something other than the mess my life had become."

"Our lives. Our lives were a mess," he corrected her but probably shouldn't have.

Her lips firmed, but her eyes softened on his. "I never considered that your world had turned upside down, too. As far as I was concerned you took off, fancy free, with no obligations other than coming back to see Josh. And paying child support."

He frowned. "I made a hell of a mess of things. I'm sorry, Shandy."

"What's done is done. There's no going back." She rose and rounded the island. "Thanks for the food. I needed it." With that, she walked out of the kitchen and up the stairs to bed. But she didn't stomp across the floor overhead. He counted that as a win.

ON THURSDAY EVENING, at Welcome Elementary, Shandy allowed Justin to walk with her to the back of the gym. His hand on her back burned through her wool coat but shrugging him off seemed unnecessarily cruel. He meant no harm, something she'd come to understand over the last few days.

True to his word, Justin had been helpful this week. He'd cleaned her gutters after seeing them full of debris as he'd strung the Christmas lights. He'd taken a couple of worn-out washers to the scrap metal yard for recycling. She hadn't had to ask, which was a refreshing change.

He'd provided take-out last night when she'd come home late after manning the counter at one of her Bellingham locations. That touch on his shoulder had been automatic, a holdover from previous, happier, times. She sighed.

This close proximity could become a problem.

In her peripheral vision she caught a hand waving. Elle and Logan were here, too.

"Isn't that Logan and Elle? They have room in their row."

Elle, in her 'manage everything' way, was already on her feet, asking her seat neighbors to shuffle down so Shandy and Justin could sit next to them.

When they'd excused themselves along the row of other parents, Elle stood again. "Take my seat, Justin. You can sit next to Logan."

Shandy grinned as Elle plunked down beside a bemused Justin, providing a barrier between Shandy and the oaf. As soon as everyone settled, Elle leaned in, giving her shoulder to Justin so she could whisper without being overheard.

"How are things?" She tilted her head to indicate Justin at her back.

"Okay," she responded in a whisper. Surprisingly, she meant it. They'd opened up during her quick meal last night. "We talked a bit last night."

"He trying to seduce you?"

"I doubt he'd try. I've got my shields up and he knows it."

"Good."

But talking with him had felt normal. They'd been at loggerheads for so long.

"I was exhausted last night and didn't have the energy to spar with him. He didn't take advantage, though." He probably could have. Instead, he'd listened to her, asked simple questions and been kind. She'd explained that she'd expanded her business, visited her mom regularly, and had provided well for their son. Josh had all the support a boy could need from both parents and was turning into a respectful, helpful young man.

"Be careful," Elle murmured and gave her knee a squeeze. "We'll talk more soon." Then she stood and stared pointedly at Justin until he slid over next to Shandy.

"Yikes," he whispered. "She's scary."

"She's a wonderful friend," Shandy said with a smirk.

Justin had his phone out for photos. The folding chairs were placed close together and she felt the heat of his thigh next to hers. Not that he was manspreading; he was solidly built. Their shoulders brushed and the scent of his cologne wafted past her nose whenever he shifted. Which was a lot. Justin wasn't big on sitting still.

The man on her other side moved a lot, too, but she barely felt it. Justin was so broad shouldered he took up more room and spilled over into her personal space. Not his fault he was a big man. Must be all that time spent outdoors in the winery.

His phone vibrated and he looked apologetic as he took the call. "Camden here. Oh, hi. Let me get to somewhere quiet." He rose and left his seat for the back wall of the auditorium. She refused to wonder who would call him after work hours. Or why he felt it necessary to take the call in the first place.

Could be a woman.

Could be his boss.

Or a friend. But if it were Jake calling, Justin would have used his name and promised to call back later.

But she wasn't wondering who'd called. Not at all. She didn't care. At all. Not one bit.

She supposed it could have been his work. Justin was the Operations Manager at a huge winery in California. He'd worked hard to get where he was. But since he'd left, she'd refused to ask about his work life and career and had stuck stubbornly to that decision in the time he'd been visiting. After their conversation last night about her business expansion, she understood he'd made the same choice. They'd parted on so many levels. Sexually, emotionally, geographically.

A pang near her heart made her see that over time, they'd cut each other off at the knees, refusing to ask or share the simplest things in their lives. They were strangers now.

As if they'd never loved each other, or even met.

Was this what she wanted; to be a stranger to the man who'd given her the best gift in the world?

She tucked her gloves into her purse as Justin slipped into his seat again, looking at the stage. Shandy cleared her throat and turned to the stranger beside her. The man she once knew and had cut off.

She stuck out her hand and said, "Shandy Camden. Nice to meet you."

Justin gaped at her proffered hand, then quickly lifted one side of his mouth as he caught on. "Justin Camden. I've got a boy in this show. Do you?" He took her hand and shook it warmly, his eyes on hers. He looked younger, happier than she'd seen him since he'd come for Christmas.

"His name is Josh and he's ten," she replied solemnly.

"That's a coincidence. So's mine."

"Nice that we have that in common." She took her hand out of his light grip and looked toward the stage. The principal was spotlighted at the lectern and welcoming the crowd of parents and siblings. On the outside, Shandy projected a cool, calm demeanor, but inside, dragonflies chased butterflies.

The show was typical of a school concert. The kindergartners couldn't be heard for shyness, a boy in second grade choir made ridiculous faces and mugged for every picture taken, but Josh shone with his magic tricks and hardly made any mistakes at all. Well, she conceded, the time the cards fell all over the floor didn't count. He was brilliant, a shining example of showmanship. A mother's pride had nothing to do with her assessment.

Elle's Jorja and Liam were stellar with their stand-up comedy, playing off each other like old pros. They did a bit as Santa and Mrs. Claus as he was getting ready to leave in his sleigh.

She leaned across Justin and slapped her palm to Elle's in a high-five. "They're hilarious," she said.

"Thanks, they worked hard this week. Their timing tonight was the best I've seen," she said. Beside Elle, Logan beamed and let loose a whistle as the twins took a bow and left the stage. "The principal decided at the rehearsal that they'd end the show." Elle's eyes lit with pride at the response from the audience.

"They were a hit," Justin said. "Congratulations."

"Could the parents file out single file and meet your children outside their classrooms, please," the principal announced as everyone stood to leave.

"We should hang back and let everyone else go ahead," Justin said into her ear. "The parking lot will be a zoo and—"

"It'll be faster to wait," she interjected, knowing what he'd say next, because she'd heard it a thousand times when they were in crowds.

He gave her a secret, slow smile that warmed her through. Maybe he wasn't such a stranger after all.

THE PHONE CALL DURING the school talent show had taken Justin by surprise, but with this kind of deal in the offing, information could change hourly, and he'd had to take the call. Buying into the winery here in Welcome with his current employer as a silent partner could be delicate. In the wine industry, like many others, these moves had to be kept quiet. Other, larger, operations were also looking to expand which meant keeping this deal under the radar was important.

His employer had wanted an update and Justin had explained, quickly, how things were going. Slow and steady with the buy-in and the lawyers. But with the holiday season it would be tight to get everything signed before the end of the year. His lawyer's office closed on the twenty-third until the new year. He should have gone with a large firm in Seattle, but he'd wanted to use a local office. It turned out to be a husband who had his wife doing the paralegal work. The receptionist was a sister and that meant everyone in the firm was family. Their family wanted an extended holiday break.

But this was life in Welcome. Family-run businesses were the norm and that was one of the reasons he loved the place.

Maybe when the winery was his, Josh would want to join the company and the business would pass down to the next generation.

He wanted, badly, to share his dream with Shandy, but his hands were tied. Besides, he needed her to take him back because she loved him, because she wanted him, and for no other reason.

He wanted to be in her good graces before the month was up so he could share the news with her on New Year's Day.

As he walked with her and Josh to his SUV, he hoped he'd made some headway. The conversation they'd shared last night made him proud of her for everything she'd done on her own. She was amazing.

He reached for her hand and pulled her to a stop, right there in the parking lot of Welcome Elementary. "You're a magnificent woman, Shandy. Thank you for all you've done for our son. Tonight was fantastic."

"Cut it out, you're embarrassing me," Josh hissed from her other side. "Jeez."

"I have more to say."

She shook her head. "You're welcome."

Chapter Seven

D*ecember 7 – Friday*
Logan, Clay, Jake, and Justin stretched to prepare for a jog. They'd taken to running together after the holiday kickoff dinner at the Welcome Bar & Grill. There was a new guy joining in today that had moved to Welcome a few weeks ago. Logan had handled the purchase of his house.

"Max Whyte, meet the Jays, Justin and Jake. Take a tip from me, never believe a word they say. They're world-class pranksters and since you're new to town..." Logan trailed off suggestively.

"You're fresh meat," Justin finished, with a wide grin.

"Noted," Max said with raised eyebrows and a nod. "Good to meet you," he said, as he shook hands with the Jays. With a clap on the back for each of them, he nodded. "Let's see if these two can keep up."

"Ho ho! You're on!" With that the Jays took off at a quick pace, laughing. Jake grinned at him. "He'll never catch us."

"Max seems like a good guy."

"I'd say so," Jake agreed. "We'll have to come up with an introductory prank."

"We'll work on it."

An hour later, it was Max who was heaving in breaths as they cooled down. "Man, I have to get out for a run more often," he said as he walked in circles at the riverside park. "Good thing I'm a block from my place. Who's up for a beer?"

Justin laughed. "I figured you'd fit in, Max. Thanks. I've got time before I pick up my son and Shandy. We're heading to the bakery for a bite to eat. It's early dismissal today and we want to celebrate what a great job Josh did with his magic tricks last night at the school."

Logan said, "I'll make mine water. I'm picking up the twins because of the early dismissal, and then meeting a client. Elle would hang me out to dry if I drove after having a beer."

Clay nodded. "Our old man scared her to death more than once when he was driving drunk. Not something you forget."

The men nodded in understanding and then started the short walk to Max's house.

"Logan, those twins of yours were great last night," Justin said as he remembered the last act at the school's winter talent show. "I laughed so hard I missed some of their one-liners."

"They worked hard for weeks getting their timing right."

"It paid off. Those two could take their act to the internet. Kids haven't seen a lot of comedy duos. They're kind of old-fashioned."

Logan grinned. "That's exactly what Elle and I thought. What's old is new again."

Jake slapped Justin on the back. "Congrats on lunch with the family. That's a good step."

"Yeah, I hope so." Justin's heart expanded at the memory of shaking hands with his wife. It felt important. "Shandy offered a kind of truce last night. Naturally, I'm pushing it while I can."

"We're rooting for you, Justin," Logan said.

"Yeah, how's it going?" Clay wanted to know. "Can't be easy invading a woman's space and living to tell about it."

"Not gonna lie, it was touch and go up until last night. She froze me out at every turn, but something changed when we sat waiting for the winter concert to start. I had to take a call and when I got back to my seat, she introduced herself as if we'd never met before. We shook hands like strangers."

Her face had been soft and expectant and once he'd shaken her hand, things had warmed between them. "I asked if we could take Josh to dinner tonight to celebrate his debut as a magician."

Shandy had flashed him a look that he used to see daily, and he knew he'd scored. "Truce?" he'd asked.

"Truce," she'd echoed.

"I take it she agreed to dinner?"

"Yep, and offered a truce."

"Good for you. Take it."

"Naturally, and I'm grateful for whatever happened to make her change her attitude." Grateful was one thing but getting his hopes too high was another. He tried reining in his heart, but it was tough. He wanted this meal to go well. To not say anything that would upset her.

Lost in thought, he followed Max up the walkway to his front door. He came out of his reverie to see a rebuilt veranda. "Isn't this the old Jones place? It was pretty rough for years. The old lady couldn't keep it up."

Logan answered. "Exactly. Max wanted a fixer-upper and this place needed the right owner."

Max unlocked and opened the front door, holding it open for everyone to troop in before him. Piles of drywall were stacked in what looked to be the living room. But the kitchen across the back of the house looked close to finished. The men made for the kitchen to see how it had turned out.

"This is spectacular," Justin murmured. He wandered to the French doors that opened to the back yard. "You can see the river from here."

"Wait, this house was in the Jones family? As in Denise Jones, the woman who helped my stalker? That Jones family?"

Logan cleared his throat. "It was her grandmother's house, yes. That's why Denise left town for Italy. She sold the house and told the principal to stuff her job."

"That's not the only reason she left town," Jake growled. "That woman should've been charged."

"I'm glad she's gone." Justin's low opinion of Denise was held by most people in Welcome, especially after her assisting a dangerous woman last summer. "I wondered how she had the money to leave that way. I hope she never comes back," Justin said as Max held up a beer and an empty water glass.

"You and the rest of Welcome," Clay said, accepting the glass with a grateful grin. "I'll have water, too." He stepped to the dispenser in the door of Max's counter-depth fridge. "Scuttlebutt is that Denise claimed to be fooled by Theda just like everyone else was at first."

"And where did this scuttlebutt originate?" Jake asked, wearily.

"My receptionist, Sybil, of course."

Jake shrugged. "She's my next-door neighbor. She and Bud have the best intel in town." He grinned. "They probably dug up how much the flight cost Denise."

"And her hotel room number." Clay's joke broke through the somber memories.

"That fancy fridge has a touch screen in the door," Justin noted, happy to move the conversation away from Jake's recent misadventures. "Nice." He, too, chose water over beer. "Are we getting old if we're drinking water instead of beer?"

His comment brought a round of grunts and chuckles. Logan groaned. "I've gone from single to married stepdad and father of twin babies in one fell swoop. I need my wits about me every day."

More laughter.

"One of these days, I'll hear more about this Denise," Max said. "But for now, I can tell you, she was *interesting* to buy a house from." With that, he raised his beer and toasted. "To new friends and running buddies."

"Right back at you," Justin said. He planned to return to Welcome for good, so he was glad he'd reconnected with Logan and Clay and met Max. Jake had gone quiet with the talk about Denise, but that was to be expected, given that Denise had—unintentionally she claimed— aided a woman who'd wanted to make him her next murder victim.

To ease Jake's mood, Justin spoke. "We're heading to the tree lighting tonight. Anyone else going?"

"I won't bother," Max said. "Not on my own. I don't have my girls this weekend. It would feel weird being at a family event by myself."

"What about that pretty contractor you have working on this place?" Logan asked with raised eyebrows. He ginned widely to include the others in the information. Everyone turned to Max expectantly. Logan went on to explain. "Kaylin's got a couple of real cute kids. Maybe you could tag along with her."

"Not the kind of thing an employer should do," Max said firmly, but Justin wondered if he was trying to convince the guys or himself.

Clay spoke up from his inspection of the cabinets. "You've got a woman doing this work? Kaylin who?"

Max looked at Logan, who chuckled. "It's Kaylin Simpson. She used to summer here as a girl. She returned to Welcome to raise her twins."

Logan's explanation only added to the questions in the men's eyes.

Jake joined the happier conversation. "She's pretty and single?"

"What do you care? You're taken," Justin said, with a jab to Jake's shoulder. And so was he. As far as he understood, Max was the only single guy here.

Max shrugged. "She's pretty, but you heard the part about the twins, right? They're cute, active, and three. A guy'd have to be a masochist to take that on."

Clay grunted as he watched a drawer close softly. "She does great work. I'm impressed. It isn't easy making these old places look true." He stood with his arms crossed over his chest and scanned the tops of the cabinets. His expression grew more admiring.

"True?" This was a term Justin didn't know.

"Yeah, a house this old has settled and is no longer square. New cabinets or any other structural changes need to *look* square," Logan explained. "There's a lot of math and angles involved to make a place look true."

"Renovation isn't the same as new construction," Jake added. "I had issues in my place when I wanted to change the kitchen. The window over the sink wasn't quite level. We had to change the sill and trim to make it look right."

Max was nodding. "That's right, everything takes planning and precise measurement. Kaylin does great work." He looked pleased as he drew his palm across an upper cabinet. "She has experience doing different things, like painting and drywall and electrical and plumbing. Anything, really. Plus, she's got an eye for design and color." He led the troop to the side entrance where he showed off the mudroom and bathroom Kaylin had designed and built for him. "Logan's brother Jamie has been working with her, too. I'd say he's learning a lot."

Clay looked surprised. "Good. It's time someone gave Jamie a break."

Logan nodded. "The folks and I appreciate Max and Kaylin taking a chance on Jamie." He tilted his water to finish it. "Thanks for this, but I've got kids to wrangle and a client at four."

Justin pondered the similarity between a settled old house that was no longer straight or level and the state of his marriage. For years, he and Shandy had allowed the settling. They'd taken each other for granted as invisible cracks and pressure had built in their foundation. When they'd hit a bad patch, those cracks had become too large, too damaging to hold their marriage together. Now, they had a chance to make things true again. To patch their foundation and fix the cracks. He hoped Shandy would come to see that they still had a chance for a true and healthy marriage.

"Shandy, Josh and I are meeting at the bakery for dinner to celebrate Josh's turn on the stage at the school last night." He'd already mentioned it, but what the hell, it felt great to say it again. He and his family were going out together. Satisfaction rolled through him.

"Didn't he drop all his cards?" Logan gave him a sly grin. "I didn't mention it earlier, but..." he trailed away in a jibe.

"But he picked them all up again and kept going. Didn't miss a beat." His staunch defense brought out grins.

Jake patted his back. "That's right, my friend. Your boy's a real talent."

"Hey!"

"No, seriously. I'm glad you're here to see all this with him. It's important."

AT THE WELCOME BAKERY, Shandy saw Justin waiting for them in a booth at the back. She and Josh placed their orders for soup, sandwiches, and slices of pie at the counter. They'd planned to come in one vehicle, but she'd had to drag Josh to the mall to get a new jacket because he'd outgrown the one she'd bought in the fall already.

"We'll be in the booth with Justin," she said to the counterperson, a new employee she hadn't met yet. "It's that big o—man— who's waving at us." She'd wanted to call him an oaf, but with Josh next to her, she reined in the impulse.

She followed Josh to the booth and slid in next to him, across from Justin. She pretended interest in the people entering the shop, but she studied her ex-husband in her peripheral vision and sighed. His hair needed a trim, but he was still in great shape. Broad shoulders tapered to a trim waist and belly. He'd been jogging today with Logan, Clay, and Jake, which surprised her because Jake had abandoned all his friends over the years, except for Justin.

"Hey, Buddy. Did you find a flashy new jacket?"

"Yes, it's okay."

Shandy raised her brows. "In the store he was impressed with it."

"She made me get snow pants, too. Like a little kid."

"Are you saying you're too old to play in the snow?"

Josh gave them a roll of his eyes and a shrug. "We don't get much."

"You need to be ready, though. Besides, if we get a good snowfall, I'll expect to build a fort and have a snowball fight. Me against you."

"And me," Shandy added. "You forget I pitched for my softball team in high school." She gave them an evil laugh.

"You're on. It's a date if we see more than two inches."

"I'm glad you went jogging with your friends. But it's especially good news that Jake's back in with the guys, too."

"Yes, I never thought I'd see the day. I met Max Whyte, too. He bought the Jones' house on Cross and is in the midst of renovating it."

"That must be a big project." She'd supervised the reno job at their home years ago so she understood the amount of work that could be involved. "Is he doing the work himself?"

"Some because he's renovated a Victorian before, but he's also hired a woman named Kaylin Simpson. Do you know her?"

"No, not at all." But she was certainly curious about a woman contractor. It wouldn't be easy to get established in a new community. Kudos to her for trying.

"Buddy, I said it last night and I'll say it again how great you were."

It seemed Kaylin Simpson was less interesting to Justin. He'd already moved on to a new conversation.

"Thanks, Dad, but I dropped my whole deck of cards." He shrugged, unconcerned. Josh was able to brush off disappointment and Shandy loved the trait.

"And everyone saw how quickly you corrected and moved on. That's the sign of a dedicated performer," Justin responded cheerily.

"Practice, practice, practice," Shandy added. "If you enter the spring talent show you'll have your act down pat."

"Maybe I'll work on some easier tricks."

She shared an approving look with Justin.

"So the new guy, Max, bought the house from Denise Jones," she said. "How was Jake when her name came up?"

"He went a bit quiet, but he was fine."

"I'm glad you stayed friends through these hard years."

"You hang in when your friends need you."

But apparently not when your wife does. The bitter thought intruded. Justin didn't see the irony in his comment. Jake would have been totally alone for years if not for Justin's stubborn refusal to abandon Jake to guilt and misery. His clinging to Jake so determinedly had added to her shock when Justin had left her when she needed him.

It still didn't make sense that he could stick with a friend, but not with her. It likely never would. She couldn't bear to ask, not after all this time.

Their breakup was a mishmash of memories of arguments, her pleading, and Justin storming out. The arguments had been deeply underscored by her grief over her father's death and her mother's condition. She doubted she'd ever sort it out. But she had to focus on today, not the past.

A quiet cell phone ring sounded, and Justin picked his phone out of his pocket to check it. Like last night, he tossed her an apologetic look, and stood. He moved toward the front window to take the call.

Hm. She glanced over her shoulder to see that he covered the phone with his other hand shielding his mouth to keep his voice from carrying. A woman on the other end? Probably. Maybe one he was trying to ditch. The dark thought stuck in her head. She had no idea how many women he'd had since he'd left. How many other women he'd left high and dry?

Maybe he was starting a new relationship and wanted to keep in touch with the woman through the holidays. That would make sense, given his phone call last night. He'd popped out of his seat like it was ablaze when he took the call in the school gym.

Residual anger and the idea that he could be breaking up with a woman or, worse, arranging a date with a new one when he was with his family, meant she gave Justin a frosty look when he glanced her way. She couldn't help it. She still carried baggage from those horrible weeks when their lives fell apart. And now, to bring his personal dramas here with him? *Despicable.*

Josh was eager for the tree-lighting as any boy would be. Her son was thrilled for anything that kept him outside past his bedtime. His chatter kept her from bolting out of the bakery. For his sake, she drew in some calming breaths and forced her thoughts away from the past.

Justin looked intent on his conversation as he turned this way and that as he talked. After a moment, he nodded and ended the call. The oaf slipped back into his seat as if the interruption hadn't happened.

She was pretty sure her face had turned to stone. If she'd wanted to move her lips she couldn't. Ice traveled her veins as she glared at Justin.

"Are you excited about tonight?" Justin asked Josh as if he hadn't seen her frosting over in her seat. Maybe he planned to keep his family time separate from his private affairs. She knew some men compartmentalized the areas of their lives. Black thoughts swirled.

"Sure. I'm glad you're coming with us," her son replied.

"This year's tree lighting should be great. I hear they have a Santa's village this time." Justin's eyes lit with a teasing light. "You don't need to go to the mall to see him."

Josh rolled his eyes. "You don't expect me to sit on his lap, do you?"

"One last time," Shandy pleaded. The oaf nodded in agreement.

"Make it a good one, too. No goofing around," Justin admonished. "Your grandmother likes having your Santa photo by her bed."

Shandy's heart stuttered. "How do you know that?" She demanded in a hollow voice.

"I was in the other day to see her. I noticed last year's photo."

She gasped quietly at this piece of news. Seeing her mother was her job, not his. *Her* responsibility. She'd wanted him to share it once, but he'd shirked and that had been the beginning of the end. This was so confusing. She smoothed her forehead with trembling fingers.

"Order's up," Alyce Markham, the owner called over.

Justin popped up to get their food and she took the moment to settle her mind and ragged emotions. Tonight was about the tree lighting and getting Josh up on Santa's lap one last time. It was a family night and she'd do anything to give her son happy memories of this Christmas.

Maybe Justin had the same idea. Maybe that was his only reason for invading her home. Maybe it was just that simple.

But she doubted it.

The Welcome Bakery had some of the tastiest food in town. Simple, but delicious. Their cheese scones were to die for, and Alyce's Jamaican Sweet Potato Pudding had won awards. Her famous lemon and custard pies had mile high meringue made with a dozen egg whites.

When Justin returned with one tray of food, she went to get the other. At the counter, she pointed into the display case.

"I'll have a lemon meringue pie to go, Alyce." The teenage counterperson must have gone home. "Did I see you have a new clerk?"

"That's right. We're staying open late tonight because of the lighting but she's only here after school. Candace should be here by now to help." Alyce leaned toward her and gave her a conspiratorial look. "Your man's home?"

"Only for Christmas," she responded. "And he's not my man."

"Of course not," Alyce replied with a knowing smile.

Augh, this was frustrating.

She paid for her pie, took the second tray that held the rest of their order, and then took her seat at the table, composed and ready to deal with Justin again.

The meal was mostly quiet, with Josh explaining with some gusto about what he wanted for Christmas.

"Don't tell me, Buddy. Tell Santa," Justin said, while she smiled at her son and ignored her ex.

More customers entered the bakery and like them, ordered light meals. Candace, Alyce's daughter, and Shandy's part-time care provider for Josh, approached their table. She smiled widely. "Hi, Shandy. Hi, Josh. Justin?"

Justin gave her a wave because his mouth held a bite of egg salad sandwich.

Shandy noted Candace's questioning tone and kept her greeting simple. "Are you here to help your mom?"

"We're setting up a table outside to serve hot chocolate and cookies during the ceremony," she explained. "It should be fun with the Santa's village. Most of the stores are staying open, too. We can't miss out on a crowd being downtown."

"Where's Dayna?" Josh asked after Candace's daughter.

"She's with my friend, Kaylin, and her boys. They're wandering around looking at the decorations. Maybe you'll see them by the tree."

"Great!"

"I need to get a move on, I'm a bit later than I said I'd be," Candace said with a guilty look over her shoulder at her mom. "Life with a five-year-old girl who insists on wearing summer clothes in December can be a challenge," she said through an affectionate chuckle.

The conversation with Candace and buying the pie brightened Shandy's mood. Now, she could get through this evening without ripping her ex a new one. She'd overreacted because of her recollections, and Justin's private phone calls had upset her.

She had no reason to be upset, or to care about who he was talking to in secret. They were divorced and had been apart for three years. Her ex was entitled to a love life. Just because she didn't have a special person, didn't mean he needed to live like a monk.

If he'd stopped by to see her mother, that was fine. He had lots of time on his hands and had to fill it somehow. Maybe he'd had another reason to visit the nursing home and had looked in on Brenda. It meant nothing.

She needed to focus on the here and now instead of letting sour memories ruin their family time. Tonight was tonight and they were together, giving Josh a happy memory. That was what mattered most. Everyone in Welcome who was able, came out to this celebration, and she was determined to make the evening a warm memory for her son.

Justin ate happily, oblivious to the myriad emotions that raced through her. Thoughts chased around her mind. Men! The world could collapse around them, but if they were eating, or thinking of sex, or, in Justin's case, immersed in work, they had to be told about the disaster surrounding them.

But their son would be different. Josh was already a sweet, caring person who loved to entertain younger children. She had no doubt that if they saw Candace's Dayna, he'd pay attention when she spoke and compliment her choice of clothing since she seemed to care a lot about what she wore right now.

"You haven't seen Josh with younger kids much," she commented to Justin between bites of her sandwich.

He chewed a moment, swallowed, then responded. "Can't say that I have. Why?"

"You're in for a treat," she said vaguely.

"Maybe I'll catch a glimpse of this Kaylin that Candace mentioned," Justin said with a considering tone.

"Oh?" She couldn't help blurting out the single syllable.

"She's the contractor for Max's reno job. From what I saw today, she's doing a great job."

"Oh." Again, the single syllable. How could two letters mean so many different things?

"Max is single, too, and we kidded him about her. I wonder if Jake and I can prank him about her somehow? I'll have to think on it."

She rolled her eyes. "If I knew either of these people..." she trailed off with a mild threat in her tone.

Her ex chuckled as he was meant to. "Hey, you were involved in your share of our pranks back in the day."

"Harmless stuff. But you rarely pulled off pranks that weren't seen beforehand," she responded. That was part of the Jays' charm. They took their failed pranks in stride but kept up the pretense of being world-class practical jokers.

Fifteen minutes later, she balanced her pie box in one hand while she unlocked her car door with her fob. Her purse threatened to slide off her shoulder, but Justin hiked it up, his strong hand catching the straps and settling the bag. She pretended not to notice that he brushed the side of her neck and earlobe with his fingers during the rescue. "Thanks," she muttered.

"My pleasure," he whispered next to her ear. The heat of his breath sent a trickle of warmth down her back. She steadfastly refused to look at him. Agreeing to a truce last night had been a tactical error. The big oaf had decided she was fair game.

She wasn't. She'd swear to it.

With the pie stowed safely on the front seat, they wandered toward the massive Sitka spruce that took pride of place on the lawn of the Town Hall. She hadn't been allowed to hold Josh's hand in public since he was seven. She missed it, that sweet connection with her boy.

The Sitka had been one of two that had been planted purely for landscaping purposes back in the 1940s, but when people had seen how perfectly shaped it was, the idea of lighting it at Christmas took hold. The second tree had withered and died an early death and hadn't been replaced.

Now, the survivor towered over the squat single-story Town Hall building. The good citizens of Welcome loved the tree, no matter that it looked a bit unruly for the rest of the year what with cones and needles dropping and birds flying in and out of its branches. Some of the bird parents could be feisty with passersby if they came too close.

In early spring, classes from the elementary school challenged each other to find the most bird nests and name the species that raised their young in the tree's protective branches. Children were abuzz for weeks as the count took place, and the baby birds began to fledge. Being chased off by a determined sparrow was a badge of courage and the children wore wide-brimmed hats and long sleeves for protection.

"Remember the year you got chased by the towhee all the way down the block?" She asked Josh.

"Yeah, I had to run as fast as I could." His grin filled his face and eyes as he laughed. "I was only seven. I couldn't run as fast as I can now."

Other towns may have bigger, grander, and more expensive displays, but Welcome's Sitka spruce felt personal. Everyone felt a connection and the towering tree was a point of pride.

"Dilly!" Josh suddenly called. Clay and Mercy walked on the other side of Main Street, heading in the same direction. Dilly waved back excitedly when she saw Josh. "Mom, can I walk with them?"

"Of course, just look both ways when you cross the street."

"He's already gone," Justin noted from beside her. "But he did look before stepping out. The road is closed a few yards up," he pointed out.

Wooden barricades stopped traffic to protect the milling crowd in front of the Town Hall.

"He loves hanging out with Dilly." Josh was already holding the little girl's hand and they were walking and laughing a few steps ahead of her parents. Josh was pointing out things to Dilly and her face shone as she gazed at him. Shandy's heart caught at the sight of Dilly's adoration.

"It's good that Mercy Talbot can live here without the locals getting in her face," he commented.

"Here, she's Mercy Foster, the vet's wife, not a famous actor whose star is on the rise. To Welcome though, she's still the Talbot's good kid, sister to the wild child, Janna." Still, Welcome was protective of Mercy and Clay's privacy, and it was rare that reporters or photographers got information on the couple. They were living the life they wanted away from Hollywood when Mercy wasn't filming.

"Let's cross over and walk with them," Justin suggested.

"Great, I see Jake and Brianna up ahead of them, too." Logan and Elle strolled, holding hands, behind Clay and Mercy. Up ahead Elle's oldest boy, Daniel kept a close eye on the twins, Jorja, and Liam.

Soon their group had gathered in front of the Town Hall. Small children were on men's shoulders and the older ones squeezed through the crowd to get closer for a better view. Josh still had Dilly's hand and they stood with Daniel, and the twins. He looked happy and half-grown, and her heart caught at how much he looked like his father in profile.

She glanced at Justin beside her and caught him looking back.

The mayor said a few words about how the year had played out for Welcome and how the new year would bring prosperity. He thanked the local business owners for their support of the ceremony, the kids' sports teams, and new playground equipment. Everyone cheered.

Song sheets were handed out and the group sang along to the high school band for three Christmas songs. After Rudolph the Red Nosed Reindeer died away the mayor flipped the switch and the tree blazed with colored lights from towering top to wide bottom. A cheer rose from the crowd as everyone called out their holiday greeting.

And then she remembered the tradition of kissing when the lights went on. All around her people were smooching and hugging and cuddling and nuzzling.

She glanced next to her to see Justin looking around, too. Then because of people standing close together, there was a break between the bodies, and she saw Josh kiss Dilly on the cheek. Then he looked straight at his dad and gave him a thumbs up sign.

Justin leaned close and whispered, "My turn." Then he nuzzled her ear and kissed her soundly on the cheek. Her heart stopped and she felt the burn of his touch down to her lady parts.

Damn the man, he had a pair. It was unfair to play this card in front of Josh, but there was a rebellious part of her that didn't mind that her lady parts danced the tango. No surprise. Justin had always had this effect on her.

She gave her ex a cool smile and waved to Josh. He led Dilly back through the shuffling people. Some were muttering about beating the crowd out of downtown, while others were calling out to friends and family. A happy throng.

"Let's go for hot chocolate," Justin offered.

"Yay! Can Dilly come, too?"

"Sure, we'll get her parents, as well."

"I'll find Mercy," Shandy said and stepped away. Her friend had been only a few feet behind them. She saw the other couple immediately and waved them over. "We've invited Dilly for hot chocolate at the bakery. Will you come, too?"

"Perfect," Mercy said with a grin. Baby Autumn was in a carrier on Clay's chest. "You go on ahead, Clay. We'll be right behind you." She linked arms with Shandy. "Fill me in," she said softly, as Clay set a quick pace to find Justin and the children.

Shandy blew out a big breath. "Thanks, I need to talk. I think." She shook her head. "Justin's up to something. I wish I knew what it was."

"Usually, men are pretty straightforward. If they see something they like they go for it. Half the time, I believe it's the chase they love."

"But he's already had me and thrown me away."

"Did he?"

"Yes, he left when I needed him most. My parents were in a car accident that killed my dad. Mom went into a coma because of a head injury and never woke up. I had to be here." She sighed. "I still do because Mom's condition hasn't changed."

Mercy made a sound of utter shock. Then she glared daggers at Justin's back as they wove their way through the shuffling people going every which way. "Why did he leave? What pulled him away from here?"

Shandy never talked about it. None of her newer girlfriends were living in Welcome at the time her marriage blew up, so they weren't aware of how things had gone down. Maybe it was time to get the story out into the open. Fresh air might help the festering wound.

To Mercy, Elle, and Brianna she was a happy single mom with a thriving business who muttered under her breath about finding a decent man someday. She wasn't a woman torn to shreds by her responsibilities to her mother, son, and her former love of her life. When a man who fits that description leaves, there's no coming back.

"Before you say anything, Shandy. I have to say that the way Justin looks at you makes me believe he's sorry for leaving."

Shandy snorted. "Don't be fooled. It's Josh he loves. Maybe he's sorry for leaving him but he's not suffering any guilt over walking out on me. My biggest fear is that he wants Josh to move with him to California. I still can't leave Welcome. I won't leave my mother, not for Justin."

Chapter Eight

"We planned to move to California," Shandy told Mercy as they watched their friends and family leave the Town Hall lawn as they headed to the bakery to get a round of hot chocolate. Justin had kissed and nuzzled her ear when the lights went on, as was tradition, and her heart still vibrated from the contact. She shook her head. "I need to get some perspective on what happened to Justin and me."

Mercy smiled kindly. "I know. Everyone knows you're going through a lot right now. And I'm here for you. Perspective can bring relief."

She drew in a long, slow breath as she gathered her wits. She'd be cool and present the facts and keep her emotions from coloring the words.

"The house had been sold and Justin was set to start a new job. We had everything we wanted. He had a great opportunity he couldn't pass up. Everything made sense. A new life in a huge winery in California where he'd have more chance to advance."

"You were all happy with the move?"

She nodded. "My parents were looking for a place a bit farther south. Dad planned to close the laundromats if he couldn't find a buyer. He'd lost interest in them by then. He wanted to retire and travel with my mom." New lives had stretched before all of them, happy and exciting. It hurt to remember that part.

"Oh, Shandy. How awful that things have come to where they are now." She gave Shandy a one-armed hug in support.

Shandy looked at her. Mercy, who'd had her own battle with loss when her sister Janna died. "We were set to leave. Our house had been sold." Her voice faded away as the pain rose. Their friends and family had moved off down Main Street and the crowd had thinned to couples holding hands and window shopping.

Mercy pulled Shandy into her side and whispered. "Oh, sweetie, this sounds horrible. You don't have to say anymore."

Shandy drew in a quivering breath. "But I need to. It's time. Three years is long enough to hold onto bitterness, don't you think?"

"Yes. Three years is plenty long enough. The longer you hold onto pain, the more entrenched it gets."

Mercy was wise in ways Shandy hadn't realized. She'd had a lot of disappointment in her career and life and that meant she'd achieved perspective at an early age. Mercy was what she laughingly called an overnight sensation after twelve long years of struggle in Hollywood.

"A week before we were due to leave," Shandy explained, "my dad had a heart attack at the wheel. Cars steer to the left when that happens, did you know that?"

"No, I didn't." Mercy stopped walking and hugged her harder. Shandy allowed the hug and buried her face in her friend's shoulder.

"It's the left arm, you see. With a heart attack, it drags on the steering wheel and sends the car into the oncoming lane. He was gone before the impact, but my mom's head injury..." she trailed off, drew in a slow breath and continued. "The investigation revealed she undid her seatbelt to try to grab the wheel and help my dad. She had the strap over one shoulder when they got her out of the car. She hit the dashboard hard and hasn't woken up since."

Mercy sobbed once as she heard the pain in Shandy's voice.

Shandy hadn't meant to be stark, but the horror she'd carried around for three years had nearly felled her. And now, Mercy knew about it, too. Did it feel lighter? Shandy wasn't sure, but she felt less alone for having spoken.

Mercy pulled out her phone and made a call. "I'm hanging out with Shandy for a while. You all go on without us. I'll see you at home." She didn't wait for a response, just ended the call, and pulled Shandy in tighter.

After another moment, the crowd had all but disappeared, and they found themselves alone standing in the middle of the street. Workers were removing the barricades to allow for vehicle traffic again. They had to move on. Shandy pulled out of her friend's embrace.

"Thanks." Gratitude warmed her through. They had a past, she and Mercy, and it had taken a while for Mercy to warm up to her. But now they were tight, and Mercy had opened a floodgate.

Shandy smoothed her fingertips across her cheeks to wipe away the residual tears from her near breakdown.

"Don't thank me yet. I'm calling the troops." With that, a group text pinged on Shandy's phone.

Mercy: Shandy needs to talk. Bar & Grill. Stat.

Elle: 20 min. Kids still drinking hot choco

Brianna: ETA 15 min! No kids to slow me down (yet)

True to their promises, the women gathered at the Bar & Grill in record time. Deciding they needed a drink, and the privacy of the high-backed booths, they headed into the bar side. The restaurant side was full of families and couples dining and it seemed too public for a private, very female conversation. Add the subdued lighting in the bar and they'd have the privacy they wanted. Tucked into the corner by the window with the blinds closed, Shandy could cry buckets if she needed to without being seen by gossipy biddies.

A bowl of chips sat in the middle of the table and Mercy ordered some dry rib ticklers and crab balls to share. "How about mulled cider? We could do non-alcoholic and regular," Mercy said. With a round of agreement, their order was placed.

Elle sat diagonally across from Shandy, so she leaned into the middle of the table, squinted at her, and spoke in an urgent whisper. "I needed to get off my feet, so this is a great call. I love my family, but they can be a bit much when I'm fat and tired and my ankles are swollen."

Shandy chuckled as she was meant to. Elle was a pistol. But she was also a Pitbull when she needed to be.

"Spill," Elle demanded. "What's Justin done? Aside from the obvious foolishness about moving away and divorcing you."

"He's totally invaded my life and ruined everything." She'd had order and comfort in her routine and now it was all a shamble. She couldn't sleep for thinking of him tucked up in that air bed, his arms and legs spread from side to side. He'd never been able to keep still and had gathered her close at night, even in deep sleep. She missed that and she hated herself for remembering how much.

"That jerk. I'd like to punch his lights out for messing with you." Elle had earned her bad girl rep in high school. But today she was a loving mother and a wonderful, loyal friend. Shandy had no doubt that if push came to shove, Elle really would punch Justin in the nose.

"Not if I get to him first." This, surprisingly, came from Mercy, the one who could not afford bad press.

Beside her, Brianna sighed softly. "Jake's keeping quiet about what Justin's doing. I've tried to bring it up in conversation, but he knows I'll report straight back to you, so he's being cagey."

"Thank you." Shandy squeezed her arm affectionately. "You're the best, but don't push. I'll figure out Justin's true motive soon. And when I do, he'll be out of my life." She never should've offered a truce last night. Foolishly, she'd let sentiment win for the moment.

Mercy patted her hand from across the table. "Would you like me to share what you told me?"

With a brusque nod, Shandy steeled her mind to hear the bald facts. Mercy recited their conversation verbatim. She had an actor's trained mind for memorization. Still, her lilting tones couldn't hide the barrenness of the simple words.

At the end of the brief retelling, Elle and Brianna gasped. "I had no idea," Elle muttered at the same time Brianna murmured, "How devastating."

Brianna clasped Shandy's hand under the table and then leaned in to set her forehead against Shandy's temple in support.

Shandy reached for her cider and took a sip. "I'm okay, honest. I've kept this bottled up too long and it's time to set it free." But her mom was still there, in a bed, alone. "Sometimes I wonder if my mom is aware of time passing or if she can hear me, but mostly, these days I wonder if my dad is waiting for her. You know?"

Mercy nodded.

Brianna squeezed harder.

Elle nodded in understanding. "I know. As tough as my parents were, as much as they battled their way through their lives, they died within weeks of each other. My father went because of a broken heart."

"But if my mom's frozen somehow and unaware that Dad's gone ahead, her heart can't break, can it?"

"Have you told her?" Mercy asked.

She frowned and considered that time. "I can't remember. In those first hours and days, it was about seeing to the funeral, and watching her vital signs. And praying."

"Where was Justin?" Elle asked.

"With Josh mostly. It's a blur. And anything he did for me then is colored by my feelings now." She was still angry, still hurt, still in shock that he'd left her.

"Life can be horrible, sometimes," Elle said. "You're going along planning for your weekend, or a new home, or a move to California—" she waved a hand in Shandy's direction— "and then suddenly, everything shifts and goes to hell and whatever you planned is gone. Just gone. And you're left with your mouth hanging open and it feels like a nightmare that won't end." Elle's voice had taken on a dreamy quality as if she'd lived her share of sudden, inexplicable nightmares.

Shandy tilted her head. "Yes, that's it. A nightmare and you're mired as if you've stepped into quicksand. The more you move, the worse it gets. Worrying, waiting, talking, screaming, crying only makes things worse."

Mercy nodded, looking stark with sympathy and Brianna's eyes filled with tears.

"And if you throw two stubborn people into that mix..." Shandy muttered.

"Very stubborn," Brianna clarified. With a light flush in her cheeks, she went on. "Jake told me Justin's a mule and you were pretty tough on him at the time."

She nodded. "I refused to hear his side of it. Our lives stopped and I didn't understand why he didn't see it that way. My way." She patted her chest with a stiff, flat palm.

The server stepped up to the table, took a glance around at their four faces and backed off with a hands up gesture.

"Justin was committed to the new position. Everything was in place in California including a rental apartment to live in while we looked to buy. His job here had already been filled," Shandy admitted. "The elderly owner at the winery disappointed Justin and handed the reins over to his son, who didn't have any interest in running the place. Staying there wasn't an option."

"Justin had no way to make a living if he stayed here?"

Shandy shifted. "I had the laundromats to run," she said hollowly, remembering the shock when she concluded the old rundown shops were all they had to live on. "But no, he'd have been jobless if he'd stayed, and word would have got out that he'd bailed on the position in California." The three laundromats had been barely breaking even. Her dad had planned to close them once Shandy moved away. If events had gone according to plan, they'd all be in California, enjoying sunshine and a different life. Her dad had lost interest and had only kept the laundromats for her in case she ever needed them. Turns out, she did. She squeezed her eyes shut.

"Why didn't I understand this before? The position Justin was in was untenable, too. If he'd stayed, we'd have been broke. Our house sale didn't fetch what we'd hoped. In the end, we reneged on the deal, anyway." The newlywed couple who'd bought the house had threatened legal action, but once they'd heard the reason for Shandy and Justin's decision, they backed off. She saw them around town occasionally with their new baby.

Shandy had been the one to insist on renovating the house. Justin hadn't wanted to overspend on the place. But she'd insisted, and the renovation costs had meant they took a loss when they sold. She should have listened to him and stayed on budget. But, no, she hadn't. She'd wanted the best of everything and wouldn't settle for something more budget conscious.

As it stood now, the house value had risen enough that they could break even if she sold. Not that she would because she still loved the house. Now that their family wouldn't be growing it would be big enough to live a lifetime in.

She hung her head. "I screwed up in a million ways." Her pride in her home and in her vision for how it should look had made her stubborn and some days, willful. Justin had given in to her extravagances to keep the peace.

Elle growled low in her throat. "It wasn't all you. He was there, too. And then he wasn't."

"It's trite and a cliche, but it's true that it takes two to make a marriage and two to let it fall apart." Mercy, being wise again.

Shandy raised wet eyes to Mercy's and acknowledged the truth. "I made it next to impossible for him. I raged and yelled and hated him for mentioning the move. When he talked about his new job and how they were depending on him, how he needed to be there, I screamed at him." Poor Josh. Their son heard the shouting and ranting and blaming.

"I took my grief and anger out on my husband because I needed to be calm for my mother. I had to talk gently and quietly to her. I coaxed and pleaded with her and when that didn't work, I begged God for help. And I lost my husband in the process."

"But Justin's back now," Brianna said. "Jake feels that he never stopped loving you."

"Of course, he stopped loving me. No one could love the person I was during those months." Somehow, her glass of cider was empty. She couldn't recall drinking it. She tilted it and watched the last of the liquid slide down the side of the glass to pool at the bottom. "In all that mess, I didn't tell my mom about my dad. I didn't have the heart."

Maybe she should have.

Brianna patted her hand. "It's not too late. Think about it."

Shandy nodded and sighed deeply. "I will."

Mercy spoke gently. "If you're sure Justin coming to town isn't about winning you back then it must be about your son. Maybe he does just want to be with Josh for the holidays."

"Could be," Elle said with a nod. She slid her half-empty glass to the side. "You can have mine if you want it. It's giving me heartburn. But then, everything gives me heartburn."

"Him wanting to see Josh over Christmas is the simplest explanation and men are simple creatures." This from Brianna and her vast experience. The sarcastic thought made Shandy hide a smile. Brianna had been stuck on Jake her whole life and everyone else she'd met hadn't measured up.

"I'm the one who needs to chill and rethink my options," Shandy said. "I can go along if this is about having fun with Josh. But if I suspect anything else is happening, Justin's out of my house. I'll pop holes in that air bed of his and drag all his stuff out to the lawn." She laughed. "Did I tell you that he bought a happy Santa and Mrs. Claus for our front lawn?" She blew a raspberry. "As if!"

Mercy's beautifully shaped eyebrows knit.

Elle gave a low whistle.

Brianna found a scar on the tabletop to trace with a fingernail.

Chapter Nine

D*ecember 14 - Friday*
     Shaughnessy Tree Farm's season was heating up. To help stoke the flames, the Shaughnessy family operated a sleigh ride through downtown Welcome. Jake had told Justin this was new this year and he hoped to take Shandy and Josh for the ride.

Justin and Josh halted in their tracks as the sleigh, filled with a family Justin recognized as Logan and Elle's, rolled past. "Logan! Elle! Great idea!"

Beside him, Josh cheered. "That's cool," he said.

Instead of runners, the sleigh had fat trailer tires set at two-foot intervals from front to back to make the ride smooth on snowless streets. The sleigh had two huge gray spotted Percheron draft horses to pull it, their harnesses jingling all the way.

The Hughes family waved back and offered season's greetings as they moved along Main Street. Except for the eldest boy, Daniel, who was far too cool to hail friends from a Christmas sleigh. But he did give them a wide grin.

"We're gonna do that too, right, Dad?"

"Sure, it looks like fun." He'd see if the driver could go by the house and pick up Shandy. She'd wouldn't want to miss this. He led the way into the Welcome Bakery. "We've got to get some cheese scones and a pie. I love Alyce's lemon meringue," he said, to coax Josh into the shop. The pie he'd had when Shandy had bought it had had him stealing a piece at midnight.

"Me, too!"

A flyer on the bulletin board inside the door showed the route the sleigh took through town. It travelled the length of Main Street then turned onto Cross where it picked up passengers by the park. The route continued along the five blocks of Cross street and then back along Main to Cross to complete the circle. He doubted the whole trip would take thirty minutes, but that was plenty of time to enjoy the sights and holiday lights. He'd already seen that the Victorian style houses on Cross had done some spectacular holiday displays. The sleigh was a great way to enjoy the old-fashioned charm of the grand old homes along the street.

"My new buddy Max has put up his holiday display already. He said he'd done it up right." He pointed to a spot on the route past the stop near the park. "He lives right around there and can see the river from his kitchen in the back."

"Cool. We swim at the river bend every summer."

"I know the spot. The river widens out and the swimming's good."

"Yeah, it's great. Mom will like the sleigh ride because she loves seeing the lights every year. We usually go for a drive, and take a walk downtown after the tree lighting, but I'm sure she'd like the sleigh ride."

"I'm counting on it, Buddy. I'm counting on it."

For the past week, Shandy had been agreeable and considerate. She'd cooked meals he liked and had done his laundry though he'd gotten into the habit of doing it on Thursday mornings. He'd return the favor by washing Josh's clothes sometime soon. He didn't dare touch hers though. She'd been fussy about what she called her delicates and hand washables. Justin had a hard time knowing the difference. Jeans, T-shirts, sheets, and towels were fine, but anything else went to the drycleaner.

He'd done some maintenance on a couple of her laundromats for her and had enjoyed the mindlessness of painting walls and retiling floors in the oldest, original locations.

The truce they'd called as they'd watched Josh's school performance had been good up to now, but he hadn't found another way to move things along romantically. No more stolen kisses or shared smiles. It was like she was there with him, but not seeing him. Polite, cool, friendly enough when he pushed. She rarely started conversations unless they were about Josh.

Or what they were having for dinner.

He missed, really missed, watching television with her after Josh went to bed. She'd installed a TV on her bedroom wall and watched in there while he stayed in the living room and had the large screen to himself. *That* was no fun. No fun at all.

Then it hit him.

"I'm in the friend zone," he muttered as he and Josh waited for their turn to order their food to go. To Josh, he said, "We're taking the sleigh ride tonight. As soon as we leave here, I'll get tickets for after dinner."

"She's making spaghetti tonight."

"Awesome." He loved Shandy's Italian food. He stepped up to the counter, ordered his pie and scones and determined to get out of the friend zone if it was the last thing he did.

SHANDY WATCHED AS JUSTIN expertly tipped the pasta into the strainer and gently tossed the noodles to help drain them. "Thanks, but you didn't have to help." He'd hovered over her shoulder throughout meal prep.

"I want to. I've tried to duplicate your sauce, but it never turns out the same as yours."

"You must be missing something."

"I wish I understood what it was."

She could tell him that she loved making pasta for her family. That it wasn't a cut and dried recipe, but the love that went into it that made the difference, but that would sound trite. And, given their circumstances, too simplistic. Because she and Justin were far from simple.

After talking with her friends after the lighting ceremony, she'd reconsidered her actions during that terrible blur of events surrounding her father's accident. While she'd been thinking, she'd retreated into herself to sort everything, including the truce they'd declared. The truce had come too soon. She didn't know.

Whatever was happening needed to be slow. If Justin was gearing up to tell her he'd found someone new, then she didn't want her heart engaged any more than it was. If he wanted more from her than sharing Josh amicably, then she needed to be certain of him. She needed to be confident in her reactions and control them.

She'd set boundaries by installing a new television in her room, so that they could each wind down at the end of the day without the intimacy of sharing a couch and popcorn. Before, snuggling under a throw and tangling fingers as they reached for a piece of popcorn had led to his licking her fingers to clean off the extra butter he insisted on.

Licking her fingers was off the chart sexy to her. She couldn't afford a slip up because of a bowl of popcorn.

She'd kept a tight rein on her behavior through the week and Justin was showing signs of noticing. Like the way he'd hovered at her back as she'd cooked. He'd touched her lightly on the shoulder, talked into her ear whenever he had a question, been helpful and attentive.

He'd flirted.

That made her frown. He wasn't behaving like a man who was committed to a new relationship. But his phone calls were still a mystery. Whatever. He shouldn't flirt with his ex.

How would she feel if he moved on to someone new?

Fine.

She'd be fine. Totally okay.

She looked at him with his handsome jaw and warm, interested gaze and wished him well.

"It's love," she said. "I make my pasta with love. My mother's mother was Italian and that's the family secret about pasta." She shrugged. "Laugh if you will, but that's what I was taught."

Justin's gaze settled on her mouth and her vitals felt a thrill of anticipation. To negate the feeling, she took the strainer from his hands and swirled it one more time, keeping her mouth from lifting at the corners. "Josh, is the table set?"

"Yes. But I left the plates on the counter for you."

"I'll pour the wine," Justin offered.

She flashed him a simple smile in thanks and then plated their meals.

"I hope I get to pet the horses," Josh said as they settled at the table.

"I hope you do, too, Buddy," Justin responded, while Shandy busied herself with her napkin.

"What horses?" she asked.

"It's a surprise," Josh replied with suppressed excitement.

Whatever this was, her son had his heart set on it.

"Will you tell me, or do I have to wait?"

"Wait," Josh and Justin said at the same time.

She refused to look at her ex. He'd be wearing his gotcha expression and it would make her smile and she'd smiled at him enough for one day.

AN HOUR AFTER DINNER, Shandy accepted Justin's hand to help her step up into the black lacquered sleigh. "This is a super fun surprise," she told Josh. "Who came up with it?"

"I did," Josh replied solemnly. "I told Dad how much you like to see the holiday decorations around town, and we got tickets."

Even through her leather gloves, when their fingers touched, Justin's hand felt warm. She murmured a thank you as she placed her foot on the step. Gold paint edged the body of the sleigh and glowing LED Victorian-style lanterns sat on each corner. The upholstered bench seats were deep red tufted velvet and she felt like a fine Victorian lady being handed into a carriage.

Delighted with the idea of the ride around downtown, she settled into her seat.

Her son was thrilled with the beautiful huge horses. The teenage boy who stood by their heads had allowed him to pet their noses and get snuffled. Josh was in love.

"We may have a horse wrangler on our hands," Justin said with a grin as he sat next to her on the seat. She scooted an inch away from him, not wanting to feel his strong thigh next to hers. She could move to the bench seat across from him, but Josh might notice the rebuff.

It was pitch dark at seven p.m. and with a light breeze it was cooler than her fine leather dress gloves could handle. She rubbed her hands together. "I should have worn my thick mittens," she said absently.

Justin took her hands in his to share his heat. He was a furnace and had always been willing to warm her. "Josh, we're holding things up here. The sleigh has a schedule to keep," he said.

"Okay, but these horses are cool!" He scrambled into his seat and bounced twice before he turned around to watch how the driver handled the reins. He rose to his knees for a better view of the driver's seat and the back end of the horses. "Could I sit up there with you?"

The driver, a teenage girl, clearly another Shaughnessy, turned in her seat to answer him. "I don't think we can let you do that. My dad would say we don't have insurance." She frowned. "But if you come out to the farm for a Christmas tree, I'll take you to the barn to meet the other horses. My brother will let you feed them a carrot or an apple."

"Wow! That's awesome!" He swiveled his head toward Justin and Shandy so quickly it was a wonder it didn't spin right off. "Mom! Dad! Did you hear that? I can see a barn full of horses. And feed them, too! Can I go?"

"Of course, you can." There was no point telling him to stop yelling, he was far too happy to hear her.

The sleigh driver clicked her tongue, flicked the reins, and they set off with Josh still exclaiming about how lucky he was.

Shandy couldn't contain her smiles. Justin's hazel eyes glowed with happiness and caught on hers. His deep smile infused her with warmth. Gold flecks in his eyes gleamed in the muted lighting from the sleigh's lanterns. Shandy thought the LED lights were perfect. As perfect as this night. As perfect as Justin's smiles. Her breath caught and for a moment, she felt the urge to lean in and touch her lips to his in thanks for this glorious outing.

Again, she controlled the impulse to show him her response. Instead of kissing him, Shandy cleared her throat. She found a lap blanket tucked beside her on the upholstered bench.

"Here, this will help." She searched for the edge of the blanket to drape it across their knees, but Justin beat her to it.

He draped and tucked the wool and, in the process, moved closer than he'd been when he'd joined her in the first place. But she was too enthralled with the ride to mind. The rhythmic clop-clop of the horses' hooves put her in a relaxed mood, reminding her that the season wasn't about rushing to get things done in time. Moments like this were to be enjoyed.

"Look at the house displays," she breathed, in awe. Some of the houses they passed were spectacular with their roofs outlined in colored lights and their trees swathed in twinkling white lights. One house had retro animated elves working on toys, singing carols, and feeding reindeer.

"This is Max Whyte's house. He had a great time with his kids and his contractor's twin boys when he decorated." Justin pointed out the display that made her grin. Inflatables dotted his lawn and the veranda dripped icicles that changed color from gold, to blue, to white, to purple.

"He's new in town." She wanted to confirm what she'd heard. "And renovating the house?"

"Yes, he's Canadian, but we don't hold that against him," Justin said with a chuckle. "He's a good guy and offered Jamie Hughes a chance to work on the reno job with Kaylin."

"Kaylin?" She couldn't help prodding for more information. He'd mentioned her when they'd eaten dinner at the bakery, but any woman would wonder...

"Single mom with twins," he explained breezily. "I haven't met her yet, but Logan says she's pretty and talented. The work I've seen at Max's is first rate." Justin was focused on a display and not looking at her. "Buddy, do you see that one there?" He pointed and Josh tracked his father's gaze to the other side of Cross Street.

"We could do that, Dad. Easy." A small forest of lit Christmas trees of various heights stood in front of a house. Some were lit with multi-colored lights, and some with green, or red, or white lights. The effect was lovely, simple, and joyous.

"The frames look like they've been cut from wood pallets." He offered his hand for a high five. "You're right. Easy. We'll walk by in the daylight to check them out."

The discussion moved into how they could cut and measure the pieces for the frames, which were basically triangles with crossbeams. In his enthusiasm for the project, Justin slung his arm across her shoulders and tugged her into his side as if he had the right. This movement reminded her of how he'd claimed her the night he'd arrived at the Bar & Grill two weeks ago.

Overall, they'd been two nice weeks if she were honest. Hearing her son and her ex-husband talk about this holiday project they could share made her smile inside and out. She allowed the subtle pressure across her shoulders and drank in the scent of Justin's aftershave. She saw no harm in enjoying the easy camaraderie.

The sleigh rolled on and as they oohed and aahed on the displays and glittering lights, she enjoyed a warmth she'd missed these last three years. Without her parents and husband, Shandy hadn't had a family connection and she missed it. Badly, if sitting beside the man who left her could make her feel it again.

Ghost feelings. That's what these were. She yearned for something long gone and these feelings were remnants of love that used to be. She wanted it again, though. This warmth and joy in another's company. Loneliness had ruled her life for too long.

It was past time to root it out.

She'd been right to start looking for a new relationship last year. Just because she'd failed at finding someone, didn't mean she wouldn't. She'd have to try again with more than a halfhearted attempt. With a wider circle of girlfriends and their husbands, someone would have a single man stashed in a back pocket for emergencies for friends. A good man. She smiled to herself. Life would change for her again. She could feel it.

Somehow, her Christmas season had turned into a blues song. Still, she cozied up to Justin and pretended for the rest of the sleigh ride, that they were a family again, secure in the knowledge that sometime soon, she'd meet the man of her dreams.

Max Whyte's house had been gorgeously decorated and according to Justin, he was a good guy. Sooner or later, she'd get a look at him. If he was all that, she'd take a closer look. She settled her mind and enjoyed the rest of the sleigh ride.

If Kaylin Simpson and her twins became a fixture in Max Whyte's life, naturally, he would fall off her list of possibilities. Having Justin hanging around for a month, wouldn't help. Of course another man would assume they were more than co-parents, since her ex was living with her.

She straightened in her seat and made sure there were inches between Justin's thigh and her own. She'd been lulled into allowing remnants of her old feelings to rise. Must be the season.

When the ride ended, Josh jumped down and went to see the horses immediately. She rose to her feet and waited for Justin to exit the sleigh. He dropped to the ground and turned to help her out. Instead of taking his hand, she held the wrought iron handgrip and lowered herself to the sidewalk.

Shields up. No more being lulled.

Chapter Ten

D^{ecember 15}
Justin unplugged the nozzle of the air pump from his bed after refilling it and wished it were for the last time. But no, Shandy was still frosty and unwelcoming. He was beginning to worry that she'd never warm up, despite her occasional heated glances and fun-loving smiles. The sleigh ride last night had half-convinced him that she was coming around.

They'd laughed and shared more than a couple of moments of family joy; between each other and with Josh. Shandy's laughter and amused, friendly glances had been genuine. She'd cuddled into his side the way she used to.

And then, for no reason he could understand, she'd gone frosty as an icicle. It was as if she regretted smiling at him. How could a guy make any headway when she seemed determined to shut him out?

Of course he'd been a jerk back when their lives fell apart. But did that mean there was no room for change between them now?

Confusion reigned, but he knew one thing. They had to clear the air. Maybe he'd been wrong to keep his plan quiet for this long. Maybe he'd been wrong to force his way into the house and her life. The only way to know was to be more open.

Last night, they'd made a plan to visit Shaughnessy Tree Farm to cut a Christmas tree today, but first he had an errand to run. He'd prefer to keep it to himself, so he was up early and heading out before Shandy and Josh woke up.

With a sigh of regret for leaving them before he could broach his idea to clear the air, he put the air pump back in its box and accepted that he'd be using it again.

The house held the sleepy quality of early morning. He walked quietly, avoiding squeaky floorboards as he entered the kitchen. He set up the coffee machine for half a carafe for Shandy before he headed out the front door, closing it behind him with a soft snick.

He needed to visit someone. First, though, he'd grab a quick breakfast with Jake before heading to the Welcome Nursing Home.

It was time to face his past. First with a visit to Old Man Sorenson in the senior's apartments at the home and then he'd see Brenda. Nursing Home was an old-fashioned name for a state-of-the-art facility. Welcome didn't like newfangled terms like Rehabilitation Center, or Long-Term Care or Assisted Living.

But, Brenda, his mother-in-law, needed nursing and there was nothing wrong with telling the truth. He'd stopped in a time or two on his way by the building to see how she was. He was careful to go on the day after Shandy visited, so there'd be no chance of her seeing him there. He'd let it slip about seeing the photo of Josh on Santa's knee, but Shandy hadn't pursued the conversation.

Today he planned to talk to Brenda. Be open and honest. He only hoped she was able to hear him and to listen. He hoped if she heard him, she'd have a measure of peace. But he needed to clear the air between them first or he'd never get it right with Shandy.

Brenda had been a good wife, mom, and grandmother. She'd liked Justin as soon as they'd met, him a skinny kid and her with an amused eye on him. They'd shared a sense of humor and often grinned at each other across a room, as they got each other's jokes. Brenda didn't deserve to lie in a bed wondering what had gone wrong between him and her daughter. If she could process thoughts, he wanted them to be gentle ones, not frustrated, confused memories.

First, breakfast with Jake. He slapped on a smile when he saw his buddy on the street outside the bakery. Jake clapped him on the back. "How was the sleigh ride? Was Shandy into it?"

"It was good, really good for a while. But the moment I handed Shandy down to the sidewalk when the ride was over, it was *over*. She cooled off again as if she hadn't let me keep my arm around her shoulders or shared some laughs." He frowned, still confused.

"That's a shame, but small steps, I guess. She hasn't kicked you to the curb yet. That must mean something." Jake held the door for a woman with two little boys in tow and once they'd exited, Justin entered.

"Those boys looked like twins," Jake commented. They both leaned back out the door to confirm their suspicions. "Yep, I'd say that's most likely Kaylin Simpson." They watched her walk away toward an old pick up.

"Logan was right. She is pretty, and she's dressed for construction," Justin said. She wore a toolbelt and steel-toed boots. Her jeans had seen better days and over her plaid shirt, she wore a denim jacket with a jaunty red scarf. The boys with her looked like happy, active handfuls. On the truck dashboard sat a pink hard hat.

"She must be dropping the kids at daycare."

"We gotta come up with a prank." Justin looked at his partner in crime.

"Yup." Jake laughed. "We have to step lightly, though. We don't know Max well."

"He's a good guy. Plus, he's been warned."

The yeasty warm scent of baking bread wafted out to where they stood in the open doorway and made his stomach growl.

"I love this place," he said with gusto. "You're buying," he quipped and took a stool at the counter that spanned the front window. He wanted the distraction of people-watching, and the window counter had the best view. The place was busy for breakfast take-out at this time of the morning. They'd see everyone who came and went.

Watching the world go by was better than running over his dialog with Brenda again and again. He wasn't sure what he'd say or how he'd say it, but he figured spontaneity would sound more honest and he needed to be honest.

Not even Jake was aware of what he had in mind. Not yet. He'd get his friend's take on his plan soon enough.

A few minutes later, Jake slid a tray in front of him. On the tray, like a beckoning siren sat two perfect cappuccinos and two cheese scones. From the scent of them, the scones were still warm from the oven. His mouth watered. "Perfect."

After a moment of first bites and appreciation, Jake spoke. "Hit me with it. This must be important if you got me up at the butt crack of dawn to meet up. I left a warm bed and a hot wife to be here for you."

"Brianna's happy to have the bed to herself," Justin said. "I'm surprised a lovely woman like her would expose herself to an unwashed brute like you."

Jake snorted. "I wash. But my shifts make for restless nights sometimes. Not to mention I still get an occasional nightmare from the summer. When I saw that fire and thought Brianna was in there, I almost lost it." Firefighters had to pull him back from going into a mobile home that was seconds from full collapse.

Justin passed a palm across his best friend's shoulder in comfort. "She's safe. You're safe. Not to mention that she's sleeping in your bed right now. Maybe I shouldn't have called you away."

"Nah. I'm good. We're good. Life is good." Jake grinned. "Better than I deserve." He sipped his cappuccino.

Justin turned serious. "Speaking of deserving people, I need to apologize to Brenda for leaving the way I did. She deserves to know I'm back and what I hope to do. I'm heading over to see her when I finish this."

Jake straightened and gawked at him. Then he closed his mouth and nodded. "Good plan."

"Will she hear me?" Justin asked because Jake was a paramedic and he'd seen plenty of weird medical stuff.

Jake rubbed his chin. "Yeah, maybe. They say hearing is the last thing to go and I've heard stories about conversations being heard in rigs when the patient's pretty much flatlined. So, it wouldn't hurt to talk to her."

He felt a hard palm on his shoulder. Jake's bedside manner in full force. His eyes bored into Justin's sending him streams of confidence.

"I need to clear my conscience. If she can hear me, I want to tell her why I did what I did." Shandy would've given Brenda her version of the events that tore their family apart. Not that he blamed Shandy, because he was the one who left. But there were compelling reasons for him to go. He hung his head as he recalled the arguments, the pleading both he and Shandy did, the deliberate misunderstanding they'd both played with.

"Not gonna be easy, my friend. But you need to have this conversation with Shandy." Jake had told him at the time to slow down and reconsider before he did something rash, but Justin had blown him off. He'd been bullheaded and told Jake to back off.

He should have listened to his oldest friend, but he'd been past hearing anything. All he'd seen was his future slipping away. His new job, his money, his wife, and son. He'd tried too hard to hold onto all of it.

"I'll get to where I can tell her," he vowed. "Right now, she's not ready to hear it. She needs to see me around more; needs to see me beg more before she softens up enough." He understood and he didn't blame her.

"Yeah, I get that. Groveling is not easy, but that's the right thing to do." Jake took a sip of his drink. "Back to your mother-in-law. Don't expect any response from Brenda. She's been off life support for a long time and..."

But Jake didn't have to finish because Justin already knew this conversation would be one-sided. Still, it would be his side of the story being told without interruption and might do him and her some good.

"MR. SORENSON." JUSTIN said, shocked at the changes four years had brought to his former employer. He sat in his recliner, his face drawn and skin pale for a man who'd spent his life outdoors. His cheeks had hollowed, and his face was bristled where he'd missed spots shaving. Food stains colored his worn sweater into a patchwork.

He'd been Old Man Sorenson to everyone at the Welcome Winery, but it had been a nod to the man's pride in his son, Sven. The story was that as soon as the baby was born, he'd started using the nickname Old Man and it had stuck, even though he'd been only thirty-two.

His pride in Sven had no bounds. The boy could do no wrong. But Justin knew differently since they'd been at Welcome High at the same time. Sven's early adulthood had been marred by DUIs.

But he allowed that his personal reaction to being overlooked for promotion may color his memories. After being promised for years that he'd one day run the winery, Justin had been shut out in favor of Sven, a man who'd never shown initiative or interest.

Old Man Sorenson lived in the senior's apartments section of the Welcome Nursing Home. He wasn't ready for full-time care, but not able to live on his own. He'd had a stroke a couple of years back and this was the first time Justin had seen him. The stroke had left him with few signs of damage.

They hadn't laid eyes on each other in over four years. Ever since the winery had been passed on to Sven, who'd run it into the ground with every wrong decision and every turn at the blackjack table. Justin had hung on for a year, ready and willing to offer help and advice, but Sven had never asked.

"Justin, it's good of you to come." The old man's eyes clouded with an emotion Justin couldn't read, but his face was welcoming. "It can't be easy after what I did." He lowered the footrest of his recliner and sat up straight.

"Take a seat," he said with a wave to indicate a two-seater sofa. "I can make coffee if you want. That's about all I can manage these days. They don't want me turning on the stove anymore." He shrugged. "Never was much of a cook, so it's no skin off my nose. I go for my meals down the hall with the other old codgers."

"They feed you well?"

"Sure. Meals are fine. If I want extra gravy, they give it to me." He chuckled. "That's what my life is now. Meals, meds, and game shows."

Loneliness filled in the blanks and a spurt of sympathy shot through Justin. "Sven stops in though. He's regular with his visits?" He didn't ask about Mrs. Svenson. Their marriage had been legendary for its volatility. No wonder Sven had his problems early on.

"Sven stops in when he remembers. Or if he needs a signature. Which is how I came to know about your offer. Best news I've had in years." He nodded, looking happy. "I never should've put Sven in charge. I should've seen his weaknesses and poor decision making. You tried to warn me, but I couldn't see it. The wife did though. I thought she was wrong and didn't shy away from saying so." He gave Justin a look from under his brows.

Sorenson raised his hands in supplication. "Not that my son's a bad guy, he's just not cut out for business. I forced it on him."

Shocked by the insight, Justin gaped.

"Sven wanted to want the business, to please me." The old man's took on a melancholy tone. "But we lived with blinders on. He's not the young man I expected him to be, or the man he wanted to be. Took a few years to come to terms with the real Sven." He cleared his throat. "He's quit gambling now that he's free to pursue his real passion. He's a sculptor, a talented one. Sven deserves to give it a shot."

Justin nodded, unsurprised. Sven had been embarrassed by his artistic ability and hated having his talent pointed out. With a father forcing his own expectations on him, it was no surprise Sven waited until now to be the man he wanted to be.

"Is this why you called me to come see you? To tell me you're happy with me taking over?"

"Yes." His gaze hit the floor. "That and to apologize for whatever happened between you and your lovely wife. I see now that as things played out, you needed stability, and I pulled the rug out from under you."

"You always said the winery was a family-run business. I should have—."

"No," the old man interjected. "I made you believe you were part of the family. I did that to secure your loyalty. And, Justin, you're the most loyal employee I ever had. This whole mess never should've happened."

Loyal. He had an ex-wife who would argue the point.

He patted the old man's hand where it lay on his knee. "We'll get this sorted; you'll see. Sven will be happy, and I'll get my life back on track. I'm staying with my wife and son for the month while we tie up the details of the deal."

"That's good. I hope you can repair the damage. Tell your wife I'm sorry, too."

"Sure."

Personal details out of the way, Sorenson's expression changed, and Justin recognized an echo of the businessman he remembered. "Your boss is backing you?"

"A silent partner. We've agreed I'll pay him out over time. If I fail, the place will be his in fifteen years." In the wine business, success came slowly. Grapes had to grow; wine had to age. Decisions were made years before results could be tallied.

Sorenson nodded. "I had reports coming in from a couple of people. The vines should be okay. That's something."

"Good. I haven't seen them since the summer when Sven called. I'll take another look this week. I wanted to see you first."

"You'll save what's left of what I worked for." It wasn't a question and Justin saw a remnant of the man he'd been.

"I'll do my best," Justin promised. He hoped he could save what remained of his family at the same time.

If he saw a tear in the old man's eye, it was one of joy. Time to take his leave.

"I'm also here to see my mother-in-law." He said it breezily.

"She's still here?"

At his nod, Sorenson grunted. "Poor woman. Makes a man grateful for small mercies."

"BRENDA, IT'S ME, JUSTIN. Your son-in-law." He waited for a moment, hoping to see something, even a twitch, to indicate she felt him there. Nothing. But then, she'd been a quiet woman, contained and careful. If she were aware in some way of what had happened since the accident, she likely didn't trust him anymore anyway.

He couldn't blame her. He'd abandoned the woman he loved and his only child. Her daughter and grandson.

"I'm here to say I'm sorry," he breathed the words on a deep exhale. "I should have found a way to stay in Welcome. To stay with Shandy and Josh. And you."

A muscle twitched near her eye.

"I hope you can hear me. Jake— you remember my buddy? — Jake Morrow, the paramedic." He was making a hash of this, taking her mind down paths that would only cloud things. *Stick to the point!* "Anyway, he says you might be able to hear me.

"Please understand that at the time of your accident, we expected you to wake up. We wanted you here with us, living a life with *us*. But as the days and weeks dragged on, our hope sank. We failed. *I* failed to hold on for you."

He squeezed her fingertips. They were cool, dry, and soft. He remembered her hands patting Josh's back to get him to burp and how content she'd looked when he did. He dragged in a breath. She'd loved being a grandmother and when Josh had turned one, had hinted that she'd enjoy it all over again. The timing hadn't seemed right, though. He'd been so busy at work, so focused on getting promoted, that he wanted to put off having a second child.

"When I couldn't get my old job back and the winery in Sonoma gave me a deadline to start my job or lose it, I had to go. There was no other way to pay the bills, to take care of my wife and son. Everything you and Sam built disappeared into your care." He hated being blunt, but Brenda was a practical woman and she'd appreciate honesty.

The only thing left standing of the family business had been three rundown laundromats and Justin hadn't seen a future there. But from sheer determination, and despite reeling from the terrible things happening in her life, Shandy had made them work.

"Your daughter's a powerhouse, Brenda. You'd be proud of her. The work she's done building up Wash'n'Suds is nothing short of amazing. I doubt she's told you, but she's doubled the outlets, increased the services and has a good staff."

Once the original locations became profitable again, she'd added a fourth. By then Shandy hadn't needed his financial support to live on. They'd agreed she'd put his checks into Josh's college fund. They had some catching up to do with it, given the time there'd been nothing extra as they'd tightened their belts. They'd made it work despite going through a divorce.

A divorce she'd asked for. He wondered now if that had been a last-ditch effort to make him see reason. He hadn't wanted a divorce, but he'd agreed to it. He'd wanted her to come to her senses and move to the Sonoma Valley with him. He'd pleaded with her to bring Brenda; had researched care facilities, but she'd refused.

"We were both too stubborn for our own good," he continued, doing his best to keep the pain out of his voice. "Each of us determined to have our way." He patted her hand gently. "Shandy couldn't leave you and she refused to move you away from Welcome. Away from Sam, too. Believe me, I asked.

"All of this is to lead up to today. It's been three years, and now, I want to come back permanently. I want my wife and my son and more children."

He sighed, long and hard. "Brenda, if you wake up, you'll have those extra grandkids you wanted. I'll do everything I can to make up for my stupid stubborn pride." He'd been in an impossible position, but things had changed and suddenly, the possibilities in his future beckoned like gold nuggets. Everything he said to Brenda was true. He wanted more children and he wanted to have them with Shandy.

He hung his head, letting emotion overcome him. Something wet seeped out from between his eyelids, but he didn't sob the way he wanted to. He wasn't a kid, he wasn't overwrought, he wasn't begging for a miracle. But he set his forehead to her shoulder and prayed.

"It's worth fighting for, Brenda," he mumbled into the sheet that covered her. He felt a movement and raised his head. Brenda had rolled her head to the left so that if her eyes were open, she'd see him. Her expression hadn't changed and there'd been no movement in her hands or fingers.

He'd ask a nurse at the desk on the way out if Brenda moving like this meant anything. He hoped it did. He hoped it meant she'd heard him and forgave him.

That would be a start.

Chapter Eleven

Shandy stepped into the shower and squeezed body wash onto her shower puff. Justin had disappeared first thing in the morning. She was an early riser, which meant he must have been out the door before dawn. She frowned and scrubbed extra hard. Not her business, and she shouldn't care. Still, he could have left a note. At least he'd left fresh coffee for her.

If he'd forgotten their planned visit to Shaughnessy Tree Farm, then who was she to remind him? If he was blowing off the visit, then he was also blowing off time with Josh and the uncharitable side of her wanted it to happen. The other side, the motherly side, didn't want Josh disappointed.

She washed her hair and by the time the lather had gone down the drain, she felt calmer. Her ex had his secrets and she had hers. Like her plan to start dating again. As she toweled off, she imagined having a new man in her life. Someone to get dressed up for, to put perfume on for, to buy pretty new underwear for.

A man to watch sappy movies with, on the nights they weren't watching an action flick. Someone who shared her sense of humor and cared about Josh.

Justin strolled into the house fifteen minutes before they were due to leave for the farm. Josh greeted him first.

"Dad, you're finally home. Where did you go so early? I was scared you'd miss our visit to the farm." He frowned; his eyes full of thunder. Was she seeing her boy become a man since his father invaded their home?

She didn't have to ask Justin a thing. Josh had handled everything she thought with an inner smirk. While she gathered their coats, mittens, and boots, she smiled serenely and waited for the oaf's response.

"I had breakfast at the bakery with Jake and then I visited Mr. Sorenson, my old boss."

The information made her freeze with her hands on Josh's coat, hanging in the closet. She turned her head and found Justin staring at her, his eyes bright with secrets. Was he lying about his whereabouts, or did he have something he wanted to share with her privately? Hard to tell.

"Okay, I'm curious, but we don't have time to talk about your visit right now. We can do that later."

"Good," he said and looked relieved. "You're ready to go?"

Old Man Sorenson had dealt Justin a hard blow a year before her parents' accident. The underhanded treatment had been the catalyst for their decision to move to California. Justin had found a new job, they'd sold their home, *this home*, and then more tragedy struck, destroying everything they'd built together. Anger rose as she pondered why Justin would seek out the man responsible for so much destruction.

"Mom let's go. I've got my boots on, but you're staring into space."

"Sorry. Here's your jacket. Your mitts are in your pockets." She raised her brows in question. "Unless you left them at school again."

He slipped into his down filled jacket. "No, they're here," he responded, patting his pockets.

Josh gave an excited cheer and burst out the front door ahead of them. The freeze that had hit her when Justin admitted visiting Sorenson, still had her in its grip. She gave the big oaf a frosty look. "I can't believe you'd give that man the time of day."

What possible reason could there be to pass a morning with that man?

AT SHAUGHNESSY TREE Farm Shandy and Justin watched Josh quietly approach a stall in the huge barn. Tony Shaughnessy twisted an apple into halves with a turn of his wrists and handed a half to Josh.

"Mom, Dad, look," Josh said with soft awe. Her son held up the apple to a gray spotted Percheron horse. The horse's lips encompassed the offered fruit and Josh chuckled softly at the feeling on his fingertips. His excitement was barely contained. "Maybelle loves it."

True to her word, the carriage driver from last night, Bethany, had handed Josh off to her brother, Tony, for a tour of the horse stables.

Tony had warned Josh to keep his voice modulated while in the barn. Josh had managed to be respectful of the rules despite vibrating with excitement.

Justin leaned close to her ear. "He's a live wire, but totally controlling himself."

"I'm so proud," she whispered back. A moment of parental pride flashed between them.

Bethany had remembered her tossed-off promise that meant so much to Josh. He'd seen her beside the sleigh first thing on arrival at the farm and she'd directed him to the barn to ask for Tony.

Tony was another Shaughnessy teen with a wide brace-filled smile. He smelled of cheap body spray and too much cologne. If she had to guess, she'd peg him at fourteen, just from the layers of scent. She wondered, but didn't ask, if the horses liked the perfume emanating from their handler.

Outside, the crowds milled to and fro as they went out to find the perfect Christmas tree or returned from a successful hunt. She'd seen a refreshment tent that also housed souvenirs and ornaments for purchase. For a first Christmas season, the Shaughnessy Tree Farm seemed to have a handle on serving people what they wanted.

Tony watched Josh closely. "Sometimes Bethany sends in younger kids, and they shriek," he said with a shake of his head. "But Josh is great."

"Josh knows better," Shandy responded. "Maybe you could set a minimum age limit on these visits to the barn."

"I'll try to get Bethany to see the sense in that." But the young man didn't seem convinced.

During this conversation, Justin stood beside her, subdued and thoughtful. Unusual for him, especially with Josh around. Normally, her ex would be involved in whatever activity their son was enjoying.

The air in the barn was sweet with the scent of hay, and warm horseflesh. Sound was muted in here, the hustle of the Shaughnessy's Christmas tree business and sleigh rides seemed far away.

"It's nice in here," Justin said with an appreciative look around. He'd echoed her thoughts and made her grin.

"Why did you see Sorenson this morning?" she asked.

"He called and said he wanted to talk." He kept his eyes aimed at Josh.

"About? I can't imagine what that man would have to say to you after all this time and what he did."

He scuffed his boots and looked down. Something was strange, but she couldn't pinpoint it. She sighed.

"He apologized for screwing with me. He's sorry he handed off the winery to Sven and says he should've listened to me when I pointed out Sven's ineptitude."

But they both knew it had been too late. The winery owner had put the business into his son's hands before Justin heard about it. By the time Justin spoke up, it sounded like sour grapes. Then, working with Sven had been a nightmare and after giving the new arrangement most of a year, Justin had looked for a change and landed a great position in the Sonoma Valley.

That good news was the last happiness they'd shared.

She shrugged off a shroud of dark memories. Christmas wasn't the time to hold grudges.

"Did you accept his apology?"

"I did. He's not well. Not the man I remember. It would've been cruel to refuse to hear him out."

"You cleared the air. Good for you." It did nothing, absolutely nothing, for her or for their broken family.

They'd come to find a Christmas tree, but Josh had reminded her four hundred and twenty-five times that the lady who'd driven the sleigh had said he could visit the barn. She filed away his interest in the horses for the future. It wasn't too early to find hobbies he might be interested in during his teens. Riding could be one of them.

She liked what she saw in Tony Shaughnessy. He had a calm demeanor, a reassuring voice and confidence. Being around horses would likely be good for Josh.

"You had breakfast with Jake at the bakery. What'd you get and why didn't you bring some home?"

"Cheese scones and I should have brought some back to you," he agreed with a sheepish grin. "Sorry, I don't know where my head was at."

Okay, later they'd have more to talk about. Breakfast with Jake and a quick visit at the winery shouldn't have taken most of the morning. She waited, but the oaf didn't add anything more to the discussion. *Whatever.* Brianna would fill her in if there was news about the couple.

They strolled to the next stall where a black horse waited. This one was much smaller than the workhorse, but it seemed more nervous. She kept her hands on her son's shoulders to prevent him from venturing too close. Tony stepped up and gave her a reassuring nod, then guided Josh closer. Once the horse had sniffed Josh, it calmed and allowed Josh to pet his long nose.

They spent another thirty minutes in the barn while Josh soaked up everything he could about the care and feeding of horses from Tony. After he'd learned about harnesses and saddles and things she only half heard, they exited the barn.

Justin had said little to Josh beyond a few words about how interesting the barn was and how handsome the animals were. The only time he roused was when Josh chased a barn cat and Justin explained the difference between a house cat and a next-to-feral barn animal. "They don't all want cuddles, Josh."

Tony agreed. "They tolerate me giving them a pet when I put down food, but that's about it. They like the horses more than us, and the horses like them, too. And not a one of them like mice!"

Josh laughed at that and thanked the teen for the tour.

Justin slipped Tony some money for his time. The teen refused with raised hands, but her ex stuck the bills in his flannel shirt pocket. "Treat a friend to a movie sometime. On me."

"Thanks, I will." He blushed scarlet.

As they stepped out into the crush of visitors and customers, she spoke. "That was sweet of you. And generous."

"Have you seen the cost of going to the movies lately? The price of popcorn alone would put a kid into debt."

She laughed. "You're right." Still, it had been a considerate gesture. She used to see Justin in such a different light. A few years ago, she'd taken his kindness for granted, because she'd come to expect it. Now, a simple generosity surprised her. Her bitterness over their breakup had colored her memories of him.

How sad that she'd shifted her view of him so completely. She hoped, one day, to see more of the Justin she fell in love with and eventually, took for granted.

"We took the sleigh ride last night. Mind if we walk to the trees instead?" He broke into her musings.

She nodded and flashed him a smile. "Perfect. We have a sunny afternoon ahead of us. And it'll do us good to move."

All around them, parents were strolling with their children, the youngest holding their parents' hands. Josh was way past that, and she missed it. "Do you miss having a little one hold your hand?"

"I miss having Josh up on my shoulders sometimes." He nodded toward a giggling toddler girl who had her father's hair clutched between her pudgy fingers. Clearly, she loved the view from up high.

Thirty minutes later they were in their fifth row of trees.

"Dad!" Josh called. "There's the perfect tree."

Apparently, the Shaughnessy Farm was full of perfect trees.

"That's what you said twenty other times," Justin said with a laugh. The boy was having a ball running from aisle to aisle. They'd started in the area where the trees were only three or four feet in height. But they weren't big enough for Shandy's expansive great room.

Now, they wandered the area with six- and seven-foot trees. Some had broader bases and Shandy had expressed doubt about where the wider trees would fit. She'd explained that she wanted to fill a corner where the tree could be seen through a window and not block passage through the living area.

Josh *said* he understood the size constraints, but his enthusiasm for the largest possible tree wiped out any restrictions on width.

Justin looked to Shandy for support, but she looked delighted with this process. Even she seemed to have forgotten that size mattered. Her nose was pink from the chilly air and her cheeks were flushed. He'd caught her looking at him more than once with what he hoped was affection in her gaze.

He doubted she realized how potent her softened glances were. Whenever he snagged eye contact, it lasted longer and felt warmer. *Hallelujah.* He may not be the pariah he'd been when he'd arrived a couple of weeks ago. He reminded himself that this had happened before, as recently as last night, and he'd been cut off at the knees immediately after. She could turn back into the disappointed woman he'd made her become in a millisecond.

Josh had wandered farther up the aisle and yelled back about another perfect specimen.

"He's happier than I've seen him in a long time," Shandy said with a wistful tone.

"It's amazing seeing him like this," Justin replied carefully. He didn't want to take credit, but Josh loved having him home. He was a happier kid, plain and simple.

"He'll pick out the biggest tree he can," she said as she leaned in next to Justin's ear. He turned to catch her gaze, so close. Close enough to kiss. He wanted to. His hands itched to draw her into his body and to brush her lips with his.

Fool's game, that. He needed her to come to him. Then he had a painful thought. What if she were luring him close so she could cut him off at the knees again?

He blinked and the moment dissipated like smoke.

He couldn't take the lead on intimacy. Patience would give him what he wanted. Especially after his one-sided conversation this morning with Brenda. The time at her bedside had brought home his most private dreams and wishes. Things he hadn't known he wanted. Things that were so huge, he couldn't blurt them out.

A home with his family again. More children. Shandy's babies to have and hold. He recalled her wanting to open the discussion when Josh was toddling, but he'd put her off. Two years later, he'd agreed, but that baby had been lost early and the idea of another try lost steam under his drive for promotion. Shandy had been heartbroken with grief, and she hadn't pressed him to try again.

One more yell from Josh brought him back to the present. "We need to rein Josh in and it's getting colder. You look pink in the cheeks and your nose is red. Beautifully red," he said under his breath.

She grinned and tugged her knit cap down over her ears. "Thank you for making me sound like Rudolph the red nosed reindeer."

He couldn't help it. His arm acted on its own and climbed up to her shoulders to tug her into his side. He rubbed his hand up and down her arm to warm her. "Better?"

"A little," she said softly, looking up at him. Her lips were bare of lipstick. She must've chewed it off. The natural pink of her lips drew him. They were the softest lips he'd ever kissed. Certainly, the most welcoming.

"Shandy, I..." he trailed off, unable to come up with a way to tell her to quit looking at him with invitation in her eyes. It was the hardest thing he'd done since he'd moved in with her, but he set her aside and looked up the aisle to where Josh stood, watching them with narrowed eyes.

"If you keep looking at me that way, I'll do something that might confuse our son."

She cleared her throat and tracked his gaze. "You're right. This afternoon has been a slice out of real life. But we shouldn't forget our actions can impact him. And he's the most important one to both of us."

He nodded and forced his feet to move along the aisle, leaving his wife to follow. "Hey, Buddy, it's time to pick the one you want. I'll cut it and get it home."

"Can we have a hot chocolate before we leave?"

"Of course," Shandy answered for him. "Your dad can cut down our tree and then call for the wagon to take to the parking lot. That should give us time to have a drink and shop for ornaments to commemorate the day." She smiled at Justin and his heart stopped at the happy glow in her eyes. "I saw Christmas ornaments on display inside the tent when we walked by."

He chuckled. "Isn't that convenient?"

She grinned back at him, and it seemed her resistance was melting. He hoped she was seeing him in a different light. At least, that's what his heart wanted. But his heart had wanted them to stay married and look how that turned out. But her eyes shone with affection and her lips beckoned, soft and sweet. The memory of them tore through his body and he leaned toward her.

"I want to kiss you so badly," he blurted. *Stupid, stupid man.*

She didn't blink, didn't move away. Her tip of her tongue emerged to lick her upper lip and he groaned low in his throat. "I know," she murmured as she looked at his mouth.

Shandy was killing him in broad daylight at the Shaughnessy Tree Farm.

At Christmas. It was a wonder he still stood upright.

Suddenly, she trembled, her eyes lost their dreamy look, and her gaze moved to Josh. She clapped her hands and called out. "Let's get down to business, here, Josh. No more fooling around. We pick a tree and that's the one." She was using her mom voice, and Josh straightened and gave her a salute.

Justin had hoped to hear a "me, too," on the kiss thing, but no such luck. Still, she didn't snap or snarl or storm off the way she would have only days ago. *Water on a stone, Camden, water on a stone.*

"This one," Josh said and pointed to a scraggly fourth place entry. No way would this one win any contests for beauty. It wasn't symmetrical or even. The branches looked thin and undernourished if that were possible for a tree.

"Why this one?" Justin asked as he approached.

"No one else is gonna take it, are they?"

Beside him Shandy gave a lighthearted sigh. "You're right. We can trim to shape it a bit when we get it home. The garlands and ribbons will cover a lot."

"Odd that this one is here. The others in this row are in perfect shape."

"Come to think of it, I've seen ones like this here and there," Shandy said curiously. "But I dismissed them as imperfect." Her lips curled up at the corners.

"Do they deliberately leave some misshapen trees? Because this one's impossible to miss. Who'd want this except Josh?"

"People who root for the underdog, and watch that cartoon special every Christmas, the one with the sad little tree," she responded. "It's a nice gesture that they have trees like this for kids like Josh."

"It is," he declared.

For no reason he could discern, she gave him an affectionate shoulder bump. "Josh gets his kindness from you."

He couldn't believe that heat rushed to his face. *What was he? Fourteen?* But that was how this felt with Shandy. Like they had no history. As if he'd never hurt her and they were brand, spanking new. And young again. With all the possibilities of life ahead of them. He couldn't produce a response that wouldn't be dorky, so he said nothing, just let her compliment sit in the air.

The handsaw he'd been given was freshly sharpened and the felling of the gangly tree took three minutes. Josh was little-boy impressed with his efforts and Shandy raised her eyebrows. "Well done, Paul Bunyan," she said with an approving smile.

He'd hit the jackpot with the way things were going today and he was afraid of ruining everything by saying or doing something wrong.

He wasn't sure if he should tell her he'd seen Brenda or not. Shandy had been surprised that he'd checked in on his mother-in-law before, but this morning's visit had been different; personal and deep.

He needed to consider the best way to approach Shandy with what he'd discovered about himself before he told her anything of his visit. Maybe she'd see his visit as selfish, as an opportunity to ease his conscience or to absolve himself of the guilt of divorce. He could no longer trust his knowledge of Shandy. She'd changed during the years they'd been apart. She had angles and sharp edges she hadn't had before.

It stood to reason, he supposed. She'd had to focus first on saving her dad's business, and then turning it into a chain of locations. All that, while dealing with a divorce, a comatose mother, and being a single parent.

She finished her call to the pickup wagon and Justin filled out the tag they'd been given. He jotted their name and license plate number so the tree could be delivered to the right vehicle in the parking lot. When the quad arrived pulling the half-empty trailer, he looped the tag onto the tree and then they trudged off for the refreshment tent.

Josh kept up a steady stream of chatter, for which Justin was grateful. He hoped for some quiet time with Shandy later when they could have a serious talk.

Once inside the tent, Shandy wandered off to examine several trees decorated with special Christmas ornaments. Justin and Josh stood in line to order their drinks.

SHANDY WATCHED HER son and her ex as they stood together, chatting and laughing in the easy, uncomplicated way they had. Uncomplicated with Justin would be nice. The camaraderie between them in the aisles had taken her back to the time before. Oh, how she'd loved hearing the words, "I want to kiss you so badly." Because from Justin, that meant bad was sexy, deep, and all a woman could want. She'd loved his kisses.

Once upon a time.

She'd had to bite her tongue to keep from saying, "Me, too." But, a tree aisle of the Shaughnessy Farm was too public, too near Josh. There were people here who knew her and were aware of her divorced status from this man. A public kiss, of the deep kind he wanted to give her, would be akin to announcing a reconciliation. Justin's "bad" kisses were best received in private. Heat bloomed across her cheek at the memories he'd invoked by the simple phrase.

She'd be humiliated to have reconciliation gossip in Welcome, especially after Justin left for California after Christmas. She assumed he'd go back to work, but maybe he planned a trip to San Diego to see his folks for New Year's. That was his holiday routine. She hadn't cared to ask, but it would do Josh good to know that his father would leave. She was starting to worry that Josh may be making assumptions of his own.

Another woman's happy sigh brought her back to the present. "I found the perfect one!" the other woman said, reminding Shandy that she was supposed to be looking at Christmas decorations. She had three trees to choose from and with Josh and Justin moving up in line it was time to make a choice.

An ornament hanging slightly above eye level caught her attention. Santa on a sled with red metal runners. The detail on the ornament was perfect and brought a smile to her lips. The Jolly Elf had twinkling eyes, a red bulbous nose, and pink cheeks. His beard flowed across his rotund belly. He posed as if he were about to fall off the sled backwards, with his boots in the air and his head thrown back in a laugh. This Santa wore the joy of childhood. He looked as if he loved sledding as much as any child could.

She had to have it. Something about the simplicity of the winter fun spoke to her. When she picked the ornament off the tree, her gaze caught Justin's across the tent. He stood with two steaming paper cups in his hands and the look on his face was full of yearning. She had to look away.

These looks, these out of place desires must stop. She couldn't go on wondering what he was doing back here. She couldn't fall into step with him, into bed with him. She couldn't.

She was very afraid that falling into bed with Justin might happen. Especially if he kept looking at her the way a man looks at a woman he wants. Her lady parts were dancing again, and she loved it.

Correction: hated it. That's right. What divorced woman in her right mind let her feminine side come out to party with the man who'd left her?

She'd been hiding in her room most evenings, leaving Justin to watch television in the living room. But tonight, after Josh was asleep, she'd go into the living room to talk with her ex. She had to clear the air and set him straight.

If that yearning look were any indication, Justin would be waiting for her, and she had the perfect thing to wear to send him the right message.

Chapter Twelve

L ater that night, just as he'd settled in for an action flick he'd seen
too many times to count, Justin watched Shandy breeze into the
living room.

"It's time we have a talk," Shandy announced. They'd returned from
Shaughnessy's Farm hours ago and had set up the tree in the corner of
the room where she'd wanted it. He'd been half-hoping she'd stop by
for a chat, but he wasn't prepared for the punch seeing her gave him.

She wore flannel pajamas, a heavy terry-cloth bathrobe and slippers
shaped like ducks, complete with yellow bills for the toes. Also, her face
was covered with slimy green goo that looked like it was caking as it
dried. Her blonde hair was yanked back from her face in a messy knot.

But he smiled as his ex-wife folded her body crosswise into an easy
chair in the corner opposite where he sat on the sofa. Her duck-covered
feet dangled off the side and her elbows were propped on the other arm
of the chair.

He reached for the remote control and paused his show, a murder
and mayhem chase movie full of explosions that couldn't hold a candle
to his interest in her appearance. "Okay, I'm game. What do you want
to talk about?"

Her glance shifted around the room as if she'd never seen it before.
Maybe it still startled her that he was here after three difficult years.
"You've done an excellent job with the house," he assured her. "I like the
new paint colors." She'd updated again since he lived here before.

"You're being kind when we both know I put us in the red by
insisting on the expensive finishes for the renovations when we bought
it."

He shrugged. "Old news. I'm glad you were able to keep the place. You loved it after the work was done."

"I still do. This is where Josh will grow up," she said with an edge in her voice.

"Of course, it is."

"You're not here to try to convince him to move to California with you?"

"We've gone over this already. I'd never try something that underhanded."

"We discussed it before, but now, after seeing you with him, I have to wonder what your real plan is?"

He tapped his finger on his knee. She caught the movement and her eyes widened. The woman knew his signs. "What? What are you planning?"

"Planning? Hoping to do is more like it." *Tell her half the plan. She's not ready for the whole thing.*

"Quit stalling." She squared her shoulders and braced herself. The goo on her face was fully dry now and cracks appeared around her nose and mouth. "This looks like a disaster from where I'm sitting."

"It's not as bad as that." He shook his head. "You're aware that the winery here had no room for me to advance. Old Man Sorenson was grooming Sven to take over and I was out in the cold." He should've seen it coming, but he'd believed his place was secure and his future guaranteed.

"That's the whole reason for our move to Sonoma. The whole reason I agreed to uproot our son and leave my parents behind." She firmed her lips, impatient with the history lesson.

He decided not to point out that his in-laws were looking at homes in Sonoma Valley before their accident. She hadn't been leaving them behind, she'd been moving ahead of their schedule. He stayed on track. "Sven has nearly bankrupted the place. The winery is out of options."

"I hadn't heard that." She chewed the corner of her mouth. "But I've avoided anything to do with the Sorensons." She blinked and eyed him. "What does it matter to you?"

"I'm buying in by partnering with the owners of the Sonoma operation. They'll be silent and I'll run the place. Eventually, I'll buy them out." Meantime, they shared in the profits.

"You're moving back? Permanently?" The muddy stuff on her face cracked again as her face contorted in shock. She patted her cheeks and drew her fingertips away as if she'd forgotten she had the goop on her skin. "I can't believe it." Her head tilted as if she were wrapping her mind around the idea.

"The old man is living in an apartment in the Welcome Nursing Home. He's doing okay, but he needs to be there. Meanwhile, Sven's anxious for greener pastures. His heart was never in the winery, despite both of them wanting him to love the place. He'd prefer to paint and share the proceeds of the sale with his dad. Starving in a garret would never be my choice, but it's his."

"Sven was a dreamy kid. Very creative."

"I'd say lazy, but then, I worked with him for years. I covered for him lots of times and his father never caught on. When Sven took over, I saw my error. I should've let Sven's incompetence show, but I'd made my bed and it looked like sour grapes when I pointed out the obvious."

She drew in a deep breath. "You wanted to tell me this at the time. But I refused to hear it."

"I didn't talk to the old man about Sven until after your parents' accident. It sounded as if I was begging for my job back and stabbing Sven in the back."

"You'd been kind about covering for him for all the years you worked there."

"I guess." He blew out a breath. "In the beginning, Sven was a buddy. When I started at the winery after college, I didn't think it would be for long. But I loved the business and keeping Sven in his father's good graces seemed like the right thing to do. I expected him to pursue his art back then, but he'd been afraid to tell his dad. Afraid to say a lot of things, as it turned out." Sven had been in a well-sealed closet until his father's stroke, when he accepted he needed to live his life as it should be lived; freely.

Shandy nodded through the entire explanation. "I always expected that Sven would move away so he could find his own way, be who he's supposed to be. He clearly suffered alone for years. How did his mother take the news?"

"He says she was relieved he'd finally found the strength to be honest. She's fully supportive and approves of his plans to sell and move on. She wants to buy a condo nearer the nursing home and hopes that the old man can eventually move in with her again."

"That's a shock. I thought they hated each other." She tilted her head.

"Maybe with Sven coming out and his father accepting him the reasons for arguing are gone. Besides, they're still married. She must still care for him."

Shandy rolled her eyes. "Maybe. No one outside a marriage knows anything. We were proof of that." She waved away the topic and moved on. "When will this deal happen?"

"Early January."

"So, you're not *just* here to give Josh a great Christmas?" Her eyes narrowed in suspicion.

"You could look at it like two birds, one stone. The truth is, I didn't say anything because news travels fast in the wine industry and I wanted to get a jump on the purchase. Sven came to me, and I went to my boss, who took the plan to the board. Everyone involved wanted to keep things quiet."

They'd also had to move quickly, given that Sven's father still had signing authority. No one wanted to wait in case he had another stroke.

Mercenary, maybe, but necessary. Sven had wanted to present his father with a done deal. Made sense given the old man's health.

"Wouldn't the Sorensons have made more if the business went on the market? There'd be competition. That would mean better terms for the family."

"No one could move as fast as I can. I know the place. Sven also knows I got shafted. Old Man Sorenson apologized for all of it, and we cleared the air. This is their way of making amends. I don't really care. I want to come back to Welcome. I want to be in charge."

"Does anyone else know about this move back to Welcome?"

"No, not even Jake. Like I said we needed to keep things quiet."

"And you trust my discretion?"

He nodded slowly, wishing she'd move closer. He smiled at her tactic with the green slime. "I still want to kiss you," he murmured.

"Hmph. I have a lot to think about," she said with a brisk nod. "Good night." She hesitated by the hallway and turned her head to the side. "Those private phone calls were about the deal. Not from a woman?"

"Not from a woman." He wanted to say more but he recognized Shandy was gathering intel so she could come to a conclusion in her own way, on her own time. He had to be patient.

SHANDY SCURRIED FROM the room, scuffing her ridiculous slippers on the floor because they didn't fit properly. She'd been tempted to join Justin on the sofa, but her foresight had saved her. Her mud mask needed tending and she hoped by the time she'd cleaned off her face, the urge to cozy up with her ex would be gone.

She needed to mull over what he'd told her. Back in her room she kicked off the ill-fitting gag gift slippers and strolled into the ensuite bath to remove her mask. She ran the water until it was hot, filled the sink, and then dipped a facecloth until it was soaked. The wringing out of excess moisture and the rhythmic motion of snapping open the cloth soothed her. The time-worn ritual was calming, and her breathing returned to normal.

She covered her face with the heated damp terry cloth and breathed in deeply, allowing the heat to do its magic. "Why is this never as good as a facial in a spa?" she muttered.

Gently, she began wiping and gathering mud, the minty scent cheering her. Long quiet moments followed as she rinsed and wrung out the cloth several times. There was something about warm water that soothed and refreshed.

Her heart needed these few moments. She appreciated Justin for stopping in to see her mother. At first, she'd been surprised that he'd bother, but now, he'd been showing his innate kindness again. She suspected he hadn't meant for her to know about his visit. Mentioning the Santa photo on Brenda's bedside table had been a slip of the tongue.

Now that she knew a bit more about the reason for his return to Welcome, she'd have some sleuthing to do. First, she'd ask Brianna's mother, Karen Bowler, about the Sorensons.

Mrs. Bowler had the best gossip. 'Best' meaning the truest. She had a knack for sifting through rumor and innuendo to find the gold. If Brianna's mom confirmed what Justin had said, then she'd have a handle on the situation.

It was too late to call Brianna, but she could send a text.

Shandy: What news does yr mom have on the Sorensons?

Brianna: Sven came out recently. A-ok there, though. ??why

Shandy: No reason. Justin asked how Mr. S was??

Brianna: I'll ask in a.m.

Shandy thanked her, content that she'd have the story soon. If the deal for the Sorenson vineyard went through, then Justin would move back permanently. She'd have to get used to the idea.

Josh would love seeing his dad all the time. Maybe he'd work with his father at the vineyard when he got old enough. Certainly, Justin would want to teach him the business. The way Josh looked at Justin sometimes tugged at her heart. He worshiped his dad, as a boy should at his age. Soon enough, hormones would kick in and she could see head-butting in their future.

In the distance, she heard the television in the living room go silent. Justin was heading to bed.

He still wanted to kiss her. Still wanted *her*. It was loneliness making him say those things. As far as she knew, he hadn't had a relationship since they separated. Like her, Justin was picky about people. That was one of the reasons they'd clicked right away. They'd approved of each other. She rubbed hand cream into her hands and stepped out of the ensuite, shutting off the light with her elbow.

She did what she'd done since her husband had walked out. She took the four throw pillows on the bed and placed them down the side that used to be Justin's. At least once a month she considered tossing them onto chest at the foot of her bed, so she could sprawl across the mattress and claim his side, too.

But she liked the feel of having something in the way of her sprawl. It felt normal to have a lump of stuffing beside her in bed. *Pathetic.* That space should be taken up by a partner, not a bunch of tasseled velvet and satin cushions.

She rolled her eyes at her silliness, pulled the comforter to her chin, and turned out her bedside light.

Five minutes later, she shot bolt upright, climbed out of bed and walked to her bedroom door.

She opened it.

And tossed each extra cushion and pillow out the door.

The satisfaction was delicious. *There, take that.* Sensory memory be damned. She didn't need a lump beside her in the bed.

What she needed was a man.

She'd considered looking for a new relationship among her friends, even that new fellow Max Whyte. But now, Shandy Camden was ready to take steps. Having her ex-husband in her house wouldn't interfere in the least.

Chapter Thirteen

December 16
    Brianna's text came in as Shandy pushed the last box of Christmas ornaments toward the tree in the corner. To the strains of Have a Holly, Jolly Christmas, she snatched up her phone and took it into the kitchen, away from Justin and Josh.

Brianna: Heard from mom. Mr. S is recovering from a stroke. Doing ok. His wife wants to move them to a condo.

Shandy: And Sven?

Brianna: He agrees.

Shandy: Any news on the vineyard?

Brianna: No. Why??

Shandy: No reason.

Brianna: Want me to ask my mom to check about the vineyard?

Shandy chewed her lip and looked toward her son and Justin, busy opening boxes and containers that held their decorations. Justin looked content and happy. Josh mimicked his dad's expression. Asking Karen Bowler to dig for more information might reveal a secret that Justin wanted kept.

For now, she decided to let the matter of the sale of Sorenson's Vineyard go. Her curiosity wasn't worth the possibility of messing with these people's lives, including her husband's. Buying a business was about more than Justin's ambition. Keeping the transaction quiet was the least she could do. For the Sorensons' sakes.

Shandy: No, don't bother. I have another thing to ask. It's time I tried dating again. Do you know anyone single and interesting?

Brianna: There's Jamie Hughes & that new guy in town, Max something. But we don't know him, know him. The guys have jogged with him a few times.

Shandy: Justin says he's into his contractor.

Brianna: I heard she's pretty & smart. Ur really on the market?

Shandy: Definitely.

Brianna: There's the new baker. No one's seen him around much - anti-social maybe?

Shandy: Don't want a guy I can't take anywhere.

Even if the new baker was great, she wasn't giving up her social life with her group of friends. She wrote the new guy off sight unseen.

Shandy: Please don't ask yr mom about the vineyard. Forget I asked.

Brianna: Lips are sealed. I'll tell you if she's heard of anyone else moving here.

"Hey, are you done with your phone?" It was Josh asking. He almost never asked her to stay off the phone. He understood her business often ran on texts and messages.

"I am." She wandered over to see what they'd unearthed from the boxes. "My mom's nativity scene, thanks!" Justin handed her the frayed box that held the bone china figurines and moss-covered stable. Joseph's staff was missing the tip, and one of the Wise Men had a chip off his nose, but otherwise...she swallowed hard. "She loved this. My dad gave it to her on my first Christmas."

"I know, Mom, you've told me every year," Josh commented absently as he pulled out several strings of twinkle lights. He set them gently on the floor.

Justin walked around their son to get close to her. He patted her shoulder in support. "Thanks," she whispered.

"This must be hard for you. Even harder at Christmas." His eyes filled with concern and compassion.

She nodded, appreciating his understanding. "There are times I wonder how long she can go on, but no one can say. I told her on my last visit that my dad's waiting for her."

"I'm glad," he said in her ear. "That was the right thing to do."

JUSTIN DREW SHANDY into his arms, and she came without protest. He hated seeing tears well in her beautiful eyes, but there was nothing he could do. Nothing anyone could do. "This is up to your mom. If she moves on, they'll be together. If she wakes up, she'll be with you. Either way, she won't be alone, and you won't have to wonder anymore."

Shandy nodded and leaned her forehead against his shoulder. One big sigh brought the moment to a close. She moved, clapped her hands, and spoke in a singsong voice that sounded false. "Time to get this tree lit."

"I can't get this string untangled," Josh said in a huff of frustration. It didn't look as if he'd noticed anything amiss with his mom. *Good.*

"That's because you didn't listen last year when we took them down. I wanted to find cardboard to wrap them around neatly, but you were in a hurry," Shandy said with a gentle smile. "So, who's untangling the mess this year? You are."

Justin laughed at his son's disappointed face. "Okaaay."

"Mind if I help?" he asked Shandy.

"Have at it. I'll put out the nativity scene and find my vintage bulbs."

From the floor beside Josh, Justin looked up and caught her eye. "You still have those?"

"Yes, of course." They'd been her grandmother's and the fine blown glass was fragile. "And I'm still the only one who puts them on the tree." She waggled her finger at him to reinforce their old running joke. She used to say she couldn't trust him with the delicate bulbs, but at one time, she'd have trusted him with her life. He wanted her trust again.

Affection welled as he watched her. She caught his look and took a step back. Too late, though. He was pretty sure she'd felt it and maybe reciprocated a little. She pursed her lips and bent to her task of unwrapping the baby Jesus from the tissue wrap.

Between them breaking for hot chocolate and decorating the stair railing and the fireplace mantel, the trimming of the tree took over two hours. The selfie they took in front of the decorated tree looked festive and happy, like any other family.

It was afternoon by the time the decorations were up, and the storage boxes put away. For a time, Justin had felt at home and welcome. "We've worked hard today. Who's up for dinner out? We could go to the Bar & Grill." He raised his brows in question as he looked at Shandy.

"Yay!" This from Josh, of course.

Shandy checked the time. "I'll be busy tomorrow so could we bake some cookies before we go?"

"Sugar cookies," Josh demanded.

"Chocolate chip?" Justin asked.

"Only if you promise to help," she responded with a saucy grin. Just like she would have before.

He could get used to this. Time flew as they mixed the dough. Josh had the honor of cutting the sugar cookies with cookie cutters shaped like snowmen and Santa.

After sprinkling the cookies with sugar, Josh left to shoot hoops with the neighborhood kids at the school grounds up the block. Shandy bent to slide the pan into the oven and Justin took her moment of distraction to add extra chocolate chips to the batch he was mixing.

When she whirled back around, she caught him mid-toss. "Gotcha," she said with a grin. "I knew you'd do it."

He shrugged in mock guilt and held up his hands. "I always do."

"Did," she corrected. "You always did."

He accepted the past tense. "Have you given any thought to me living back in Welcome?"

"Where?" Her gaze was curious, not inviting.

"Logan's selling those new houses near the highway. They're selling fast. He says there's a deal that fell through. Corner lot, four bedrooms with room to put a second driveway around the corner into the backyard. Nice spot for an RV or a boat."

"You? Living the suburban dream?" She took the mixing bowl from his hands and tossed in another handful of chocolate chips. "I can't see you taking on that much yardwork. And an RV? Hah! Getting you away for a weekend would be impossible."

"Not impossible when you're with the family you want."

Her eyes moistened and she stilled as she took in his comment. For a time the cookie dough had her attention as she pushed the wooden spoon through the heavy glop. After a long, heavy silence in which his emotions swung from hope to worry that he'd said too much, she spoke. "I've decided it's time to start dating again."

"Who?" Justin blurted into the dead zone between him and Shandy. She was dating! He'd been back for over two weeks, and this was the first he'd heard of it. "You could've told me sooner."

She opened her mouth, but he raced on, refusing to let her speak. "Is it a problem that I'm here in your house? That I'm hanging out with my own son? Why didn't Josh tell me about this guy? Is he mean to our kid? Does he even *like* Josh?" The questions fell, turbulent and demanding from his brain into his mouth and out to his wife's startled face.

"You be careful here, Justin." Her voice was low and tense and even during the worst fights they'd had before he hadn't heard this tone. She was too angry to yell.

He backed up a step.

She advanced on him and glared into his face. Like right up close and personal. And threatening. "How dare you question if a man I'd bring into this house would be hard on Josh. As if I'd ever expose him to—Arrgh! — what's the use? Just the fact that you'd ask proves what an ass you can be." Her face was blood red, her eyes flashing indignation. "How dare you question my mothering? My standards?"

"I—I—." This blow up was the biggest he'd seen and all he could do was spin his brain trying to come up with something, anything, to calm her so they could talk about this guy in her life.

"Make your own damn cookies!" She slammed the mixing bowl to the counter and stormed toward the front hall closet. She glared at him as she threw on her coat, grabbed her purse from inside the closet, and scuffed into her sexy short boots. The next sound he heard was the slam of the front door. Then she opened it back up and slammed it again.

He pinched his lips waiting for the third, but it didn't come. She'd left.

Justin stared, numb and lost, at the big blob of raw cookie dough. That was a lot of chocolate chips.

The scent of the baking sugar cookies wafted toward him and reminded him of what he'd lost. Not just before when they'd separated, but today, too. Every inroad he'd made with Shandy had been bulldozed because he ran his mouth. Every fear he'd ever had around leaving Shandy and Josh had come to the surface and spilled out right in her face.

No wonder she'd slammed out the door. Twice.

Chapter Fourteen

Shandy jumped into her car and drove hell bent for leather to the corner where she pulled over. She texted Brianna to find that her friend was at her mom's house. Karen Bowler ran a dog rescue and lived on a five-acre parcel next to Clay and Mercy. The drive should take about twenty minutes. Time enough to calm down.

She texted again and got an immediate invitation to visit. Good, she'd go there. Nothing worse than storming out in a fit of temper only to find you had nowhere to go. Just wait until her friends heard about what Justin said. What he'd accused her of. What he thought of her. She fought down a sob. She'd never imagined he'd believe she could put a new man above their son.

Oh, no. He was texting her.

Justin: I'm sorry.

Shandy: You should be. Pack your stuff. You can't be there when I get back.

She turned off her phone, started her car and rolled to the stop sign. She'd pick up Josh on the way past the school and let him play with the dogs out at the rescue while she vented to her friends. No matter how angry she was at Justin, she'd never said a bad word about him to their son. She wouldn't start today, either.

She pulled into the school parking lot and shut off her car. Needing to calm down before seeing Josh, Shandy counted to ten slowly. When she calmed, she honked and saw the boys lift their heads from the game and look toward her. Josh ran to the car and climbed in. "What's up?"

"Want to go to the Bowler Dog Rescue with me? I'm heading there now."

"Sure! Can I play with the dogs and see Dilly, too?"

"Of course. Use my phone to text your dad that you're with me," she said as she pulled out of the lot.

He picked up the phone and gasped.

"Oh, no. You read my last message?"

"Hard to miss it." Her son's voice was cold. So cold. But his eyes were stricken.

"Josh, I'm sorry, but we've had a disagreement and I can't let your dad stay in the house with us anymore."

Josh's chin sank to his chest. "Okay."

"I'm sorry," she repeated.

"But that's what he says in his text, and it didn't matter to you. Why should *I* care when you say *you're* sorry?"

He had a point, but he was ten, not seven anymore. And she and his father been apart for years. "It's not as simple as that. Grownups, especially divorced parents, say things to make each other angry because of lots of deep reasons. Sometimes even they can't explain why, and the words pop out. But once they're out there, you can't take them back. They sting and hurt the other person." She stopped at a red light and took the time to look into her son's face. His eyes went wide and solemn.

She sighed and confessed. "It's time I told you that I've said lots of hurtful things to him, too. There's no bad guy here. We're both at fault." She bit her lip.

Both at fault. She'd deliberately baited Justin. She could see it now.

"Are you really making him leave the house?"

"Maybe that would be best. I'll discuss it with him and see if we can agree on a ceasefire."

"I want him to stay."

"I understand that, of course. Your dad knows how you feel, too. I promise we'll look at all the angles before deciding. But you're old enough to understand that some things don't work out the way you want them to."

She felt terrible warning him about the harsh reality of divorce, but Josh wasn't a baby anymore. Part of her was angry that Justin had forced this situation on them all. Her biggest mistake was letting her ex walk in the door with that airbed in his arms.

Conversation died while she drove the rest of the way to Bowler's Rescue. There was nothing left to discuss. When she promised to look at all sides of the issue, Josh believed her because Shandy kept her promises. Still, her son gazed at the passing scenery and didn't look at her again.

Twenty minutes later, Shandy turned into the driveway of Bowler's Rescue. The white bungalow with green trim hadn't changed much and the chorus of dog barks welcomed them as they climbed out of the car.

"Can I go around back?"

"Yes. Say hello to Beau for me."

"Can I go get Dilly?"

"If her parents say it's okay." Having Dilly with Josh would mean she'd get more time on her own with Brianna, Karen, and maybe Mercy if she could get away from her house for a few minutes. Josh took off at a run, hopped the split rail fence that separated the properties between the houses, and headed for the back of the Fosters' house. She watched as he rapped on the French door that opened to the dining area from the deck. The door opened and he stepped inside out of view.

She blew out a big breath. Her feelings had changed from anger at Justin to confusion on what was best for her son.

The front door of the bungalow creaked, drawing her attention. In the open door, Brianna stood, her face wreathed by concern. "Come in. Mom's got the coffee on."

"Good, but I may need something stronger," she confessed as she trudged up the three steps to the porch. "Josh has gone to get Dilly. I hope that's okay."

"Of course, Beau will be thrilled."

Beau the pit bull was a fixture at the rescue and technically belonged to Clay, but the dog lived here. Karen used him to calm new arrivals. She liked to say he showed them the ropes of life at the rescue. Their own welcoming committee.

Brianna gave her a warmhearted hug and tsked at the tears that sparked in her eyes. "No. Don't let Justin make you cry."

"I'm so angry I could spit." She wasn't certain who deserved her anger more, her ex or herself.

Karen stood in the kitchen doorway; her iron gray hair pulled into a messy bun. Her Christmas tree twinkled in the corner and for a moment Shandy was startled. Christmas had fled her mind as she'd raced out of her house.

The scent of gingerbread reminded her that she'd left two pans of sugar cookies in the oven. Great. She shrugged out of her coat and hung it on a peg by the door. As she toed off her boots, she looked at the time. Those cookies would be ruined by now.

"I have to call him."

"Really?" Brianna drawled.

"You'll hear why." And she called Justin's phone. "Did you pull those cookies out of the oven?" she asked the moment he answered. He didn't deserve a greeting.

"Yes. They're delicious." He made a humming sound. "I also put the other batch in. They'll be ready before I leave."

"Fine. I want my den put back to rights, too." She should tell him they'd talk later, but spite reared his head and she wanted, badly, to hurt him. Revenge shimmered around the edges of her mind and for a moment it tasted sweet.

"Of course. I'm sorry—"

She hung up, cutting off his apology. Brianna's and Karen's eyebrows were raised in identical expressions of curiosity. "He's moving out of my place," she explained. "I can't bear to see him there anymore."

Karen made a moue of her lips. "Good."

Brianna looked closely at Shandy. "You're okay with kicking him to the curb?"

"I'm as okay with that as he was with leaving me." The lie tasted like ashes, because as she'd clicked off the phone, Josh's face swam before her mind's eye.

"The thing is..." Brianna hesitated.

"What? What's the thing?" Shandy coaxed as they moved slowly toward the kitchen through the living room. She skirted Karen's recliner and noticed a new one in the other corner. It seemed things had moved along with Karen and Duncan.

"Jake said Justin was torn up about the separation. He took it super hard."

"I doubt that. He left for Sonoma and never looked back."

Karen cleared her throat. "Except that he's been back here every other weekend for Josh. So, he's looked back plenty."

Shandy slammed her hands to her hips. "Did I ask to be corrected?"

"Nope." Karen looked unrepentant. "But you need to be if you're seeing him through a hard lens. He's been the best dad he can be, given the circumstances."

"I came here to get support," she grumbled as she brushed by her friend's mom to stand in the kitchen. "Until this moment, I liked your no-nonsense advice." She wasn't sure why she pulled out the surly tone, but this was hard.

Karen snorted. "As long as it's aimed at everyone else?"

Shandy could swear there was a chuckle under her words. Petulance rose and she didn't like feeling like a three-year-old in a temper. "I take my coffee with cream, no sugar."

Brianna rushed to pour her a mugful. Karen pulled out a chair and sat at the table. She slid a plate of gingerbread men toward Shandy. "Sit, take a load off and unburden yourself. But don't expect me to kiss your troubles away. It's time for honest reflection."

Shandy dropped into the chair across from Karen and accepted the mug of coffee that Brianna put in front of her. "I miss talking to my mom," she confessed. "I miss her so much." She covered her face with her hands until she regained control.

When she looked up, Karen's gaze softened. Brianna gave her a one-armed hug from the chair beside her. "Aw, sweetie. This must be hard for you. Your husband's back in your house, taking up space in your life and ruining everything."

Shandy sniffed. "He is. Sometimes I feel like he's looking at me the way he used to. When we were together and happy. And then, I get angry about the way he makes me want to go back in time." She blinked as tears smarted. "I've asked him what he's doing here, and he swears it's not to convince Josh to move away with him."

"Maybe it's not." Brianna, sounding curious.

"Last night, he told me he's got a line on work here." She couldn't tell the whole truth about him investing in the Sorenson's vineyard. That was much more permanent than just getting a job nearby. "He mentioned today that he's considering buying a house. A four bedroom with room for an RV or boat in the backyard. That spells a new family. He's working up to tell me he's found someone else." Except he'd already said the private calls were about business. Didn't matter because she was miffed with him. She shifted the load of guilt her lie of omission brought on.

"What about the looks he gives you?" Karen wanted to know, none-too-kindly.

Shandy tossed her a sour face. "Fake. All of them. He's buttering me up for a fall." To think, she'd had some warm, fuzzy feelings during some of their family times together. The sleigh ride, the Christmas tree hunt, even trimming the tree earlier. When he'd said he wanted to kiss her, she'd believed him.

"Buttering you up? That doesn't sound like Justin. He's loyal and kind." Brianna was being deliberately obtuse, refusing to see what was right in front of her.

"Loyal to his friends but not to me," she insisted. The three-year-old's temper was back. She hated it. Hated that she felt helpless in the face of it. *How long had she bottled up this anger? Years.*

"You're the one who asked me if I knew any interesting single men." Brianna cocked her eyebrow while Karen clucked her tongue.

Shandy closed her eyes. Hypocrisy was hard to ignore when she was the hypocrite. "Okay. Yes." She looked at Karen who was shaking her head sadly. "I told him that I was going to start dating again."

"Why? What possessed you to tell him that?" Karen asked. "Forgive me, but your social life isn't his business. Unless you want it to be?"

"Did you want to punish him some more?" Brianna wanted to know.

"Why do I feel like I'm on the hot seat right now? These are a lot of questions." She shook her head. Escape beckoned but Josh had his heart set on a nice, happy visit. "Okay, I'll give you the whole story. Don't interrupt," she instructed.

When both women nodded, she began. "After talking about a new job opportunity, he mentioned buying a house from Logan in the new subdivision. It has four bedrooms. Clearly, it's for a family." The family he really wanted. "I figured what he'd say next." She tapped her fingers against her mug. Without looking at their pitying faces she went on. "That he'd met someone else, a woman either with children or who wanted some. I assumed one of those bedrooms would be for Josh when he goes over for weekends."

Karen reared back. "He tells you he's got work here and that he's interested in a new house, and you jump to a crazy conclusion."

"It's not crazy. You'll recall that he left me." She slammed her palm to her chest.

"But you're the one who asked for the divorce," Brianna said softly.

"Only to teach him a lesson. Walking out on me when I needed him most. I needed him *here,* and he *left.* What was I supposed to do? Just let him go without consequences?"

"You were angry, and you punished him."

She slammed her mug to her lips and drank the rest of her coffee. "He deserved to lose us."

"The way you lost your parents?" Karen inquired.

Shandy closed her eyes against the truth. "He went to see her. My mom. I don't know why or what he talked about, but he was quiet afterward." She smoothed trembling fingers across her cheeks. They came away wet. She smoothed her hands across her thighs to dry them.

One quick knock came at the kitchen door, and it swung open to reveal Josh, Dilly, and Beau, all of them grinning.

"Auntie Shandy, Auntie Brianna, Auntie Karen! I gots a kitty!" Dilly ran from one woman to the next dispensing quick, breathless hugs as she squealed her delight.

"You did? Where is it?"

"Sleeping." She put her fingertip to her lip in a classic shush. "In my bed," she whispered. Her eyes danced with delight at her good fortune.

"A new kitty and a baby sister," Karen said with a wide smile. "You are one lucky girl."

Beau milled around the room setting his head on each woman's knee until he got the requisite pet on his broad head. One side of his face and one ear was black while the other was white. His large brown eyes were gentle and soulful.

Josh stood by the door, waiting for Dilly and the dog to make the rounds. Shandy looked at him, which prompted him to speak. "Mrs. Bowler, my dad and I are making Christmas trees out of wooden frames for outside. Would you like me to make you one?"

"Sure, what do they look like?"

"Did you go on the sleigh ride tour to see the lights yet?"

Karen exaggerated a delighted face. "Do you mean those cute trees on that place on Cross Street?"

"Those ones, yes!"

"How much?"

"Would twenty dollars be too much? My dad and I have to buy the pallets and strings of lights."

"You've got a deal. But a grouping of three like the house had looked real nice. Can you make me three?"

"Sure!" Josh looked at his mother to see her reaction.

"Josh, charging friends for this is inappropriate." She wasn't sure he should see Christmas as a business enterprise. Wasn't it commercial enough?

Her son reddened. "I want to earn some money for Christmas." He swallowed hard. "For presents and stuff."

"Do more chores around the house and you'll get a higher allowance."

"But Dad said we could do this together," he whined.

Dad said. "Of course, he did." And now she had to be the bad guy.

Karen patted her hand from across the table. "I'm pleased as punch to see your son wants to earn extra cash on labor by his own hand. I'd be honored to be his first customer."

Saved by Karen's kindness. "Clearly, you and your dad have plans. I suppose you'll be using the garage to assemble them?" she asked Josh.

"Sure, where else?" He gave her a defiant look. She'd been played and Karen had had an unwitting hand in trapping her. Josh wanted his father to stay in the house and doing this project would keep Justin in their daily lives.

Where else, indeed. She had no choice but to let Justin stay at the house. Kicking him out now would only disappointment Josh especially since she'd promised to consider every angle. Josh had skillfully brought another angle into the equation.

She wasn't a fool. Josh had noticed her and Justin during their shared family moments. He'd seen some of their secret smiles and affectionate glances. His hopes were up for a friendlier atmosphere, if not a full friendship between his parents. This is exactly what she hadn't wanted to happen. She sagged a bit as she accepted the truth. She was stuck with the oaf for now and she'd have to wait for him to move out before she tried dating again.

She glanced at the other women. Karen nodded and Brianna smiled encouragement.

Brianna rose. "Who'd like a hot chocolate?"

Dilly and Josh gave her an enthusiastic *yes,* then clamored to sit together in the dining room apart from the grownups. Karen took the plate of gingerbread men to them and for a time, the conversation was filled with Christmas and talk of gifts and shopping.

"Excuse me, I need to send Justin a text," she said, taking advantage of everyone's distraction.

Chapter Fifteen

Justin was wrestling his deflated airbed into a roll when his phone pinged with a text. It was Shandy. "What have I done wrong now?" he muttered. He picked up his phone and tapped the message.

Shandy: You can stay.

Shocked, Justin responded: Ok. Why?

He tried not to get his hopes up, but relief warmed his chest. He was still in her life. A reprieve.

Shandy: Josh says you've got a project to make trees. You'll need the garage.

Justin: Ok. That's true.

Shandy: He's a salesman. Sold 3 to Karen B.

He let out a whoop. Smart boy. Pride filled his chest.

Justin: He wants to buy you a special present. I told him to do more chores for the $

Shandy: I tried that, too.

He laughed out loud in the empty room.

Justin: Guess we'll have to get cracking if we've got a paying customer.

He was hoping for a smiley face or some other emoji to indicate her mood, but nothing more showed up. He didn't care, he was still here and still had time to wear her down. Man, she was stubborn.

He unrolled the airbed and pulled out the pump again. Fitting the nozzle to the bed, he turned on the pump and let the roar drown out his worry. *One thing at a time.*

The bed restored to full size, he checked the time and sent a text to Jake, asking for a meet-up. The reply came immediately.

Jake: Brianna's at her mom's, so head over here.

He pulled out his sheets and remade the bed. Five minutes after that, Justin grabbed his keys and left. One quick stop at the hardware store for more strings of lights and he drove to Jake's neighborhood.

They called these ranch bungalows mid-century modern, but to him, they were cookie-cutter homes on square lots. The only changes were paint colors with the occasional home sporting new roof shingles and aluminum siding from the seventies. Jake's place had a new front door and new windows everywhere because of an incident last summer where most of the glass was smashed around the house. Having an ex-girlfriend murderous stalker was hard on a guy's real estate investment.

When he knocked on the door, Jake hollered at him to come on in. Justin stepped inside to the scent of frying bacon. His stomach growled. The cookies he'd snacked on were long gone. He kicked off his boots and found his buddy in the kitchen. There were two plates on the table. Apparently, he was invited for a late afternoon breakfast. He hung his jacket on the back of the chair and took a seat. "Hey, waiter, where's my coffee?"

"Funny. You're a funny guy. No one's ever told you that before, right?" Jake asked as he plated bacon and eggs. He replaced Justin's empty plate with the full one and got his own food together. "Breakfast isn't for seven a.m. anymore."

"Shift work's tough."

Jake forked up some scrambled eggs. "You get used to it. It's easier now with Brianna here. She keeps me grounded and fed and happy."

"Marriage suits you."

"I can't believe how much," Jake remarked. "Love makes the world go round. At least for me. I never saw this in my future, but now, I can't imagine being alone." He cocked an eyebrow at Justin, his gaze contrite. "Sorry, man, how're things going with Shandy?"

Jake was new to having love in his life. To having a wife and a hopeful future.

While Justin had thrown his away. But not for long.

"One minute I think I see progress and the next she's storming off or growling at me like a wounded bear. She told me to pack up and leave not three hours ago."

"Whoa, hey. That's rough."

Justin shook his head. "No problem, now, though." He raised and dropped his shoulders. "My son likely saved my butt when they went out together because out of the blue, she texted that I could stay. Something about Josh selling Christmas display trees we're building together. I'm looking for projects to do with him and we decided on these trees. I figured we'd make three or four for the house and now, the kid's got us in business."

"You mean the frames down the block from Max's house?"

"Yes. Josh and I walked by and figured out how to make them."

"Add us to your list of customers. I like them and Brianna made noises about me making some. This would be much easier." He leaned toward Justin. "You know I'm not much for carpentry."

"You don't know the difference between a screw and a nail."

"That's a lie!"

"Okay, so maybe you know that much."

"How many trees did Karen ask for?"

"Three."

"Then at least that many."

"You're down for three, then. Fifty bucks each."

"What? How much did Josh get from my *mother-in-law*?"

"Fifty bucks each."

"I can't tell if you're answering my question or just repeating the price you pulled out of your butt."

Justin shrugged. "Take it or leave it." He fought to control a grin.

Jake nodded. "Okay. As long as the profit goes to Josh."

"Done." He'd take Josh to the hardware store for more supplies after school tomorrow. He had to see Sven in the morning to go over some details for the transfer of the business, but his afternoon would be about hanging with Josh. "I need to make a list of people who may want some. We've got nine days to Christmas."

"What set Shandy off this morning? Why'd she want to kick you out? What'd you say?"

"You assume it's my fault?"

"Yeah, of course it was."

He drew a deep breath, and then let it out slowly. "I sort of blew my stack, too. She mentioned she's dating, and I lost it. We were having a great morning trimming the tree, baking cookies together. Then Josh left to shoot hoops with his friends, and we were alone. I figured I'd warm her up by telling her about a house out in the new subdivision. Logan showed me the place yesterday. It would be great for us three and maybe a couple more kids, if we're lucky."

"Wow! You've walked a long way on that yellow-brick road of yours."

His face heated. "That's what I want. To pick things up, clear the air, and get back what we lost. Shandy and I belong together. I can't say it or see it any other way."

"Back up a bit. You said she's dating?"

He slumped into his chair. "Apparently." He went over, in detail, what she'd said, but all that came clear was how he'd responded. Listening to his explanation, he saw how angry he'd been at the idea of another man being in Josh's life. "Josh never said anything about a guy hanging around. You'd think he'd have mentioned it."

Jake nodded like a bull ready to charge; slowly, warily, as if he had to weigh his words. "Because according to Brianna, there isn't a guy in Shandy's life. She told me Shandy hasn't dated in a couple of years. She's been focused on her business and Josh, and that's all."

Justin's gut dropped to the floor when he recalled the accusations he'd thrown at her. "They're good friends. Brianna would be aware if there was someone in Shandy's life. But maybe she wouldn't tell you." It was a statement, but the tone was questioning. He needed reassurance. *Pitiful.*

If there was a guy, Shandy never would've let Justin stay in the den. His mouth went dry. If she cared for another man, Justin would be out in the cold.

Also, she'd have a babysitter on speed dial if she were dating. The only one she used to cover evenings was Candace and that meant a return home by ten o'clock or so. Hardly the hours a dating couple would keep.

"I'm an ass," Justin announced, feeling lower with every heartbeat.

"You're just learning this now?" Jake picked up their empty plates and took them to the sink. "Does this mean you have crow to eat?"

"Wonder how good it is roasted," he muttered. "No wonder she booted me out."

"You need to thank your boy, too. He saved your butt and unknowingly kept you in the house. Although Josh is a smart kid, maybe he worked a way around his mom to save your butt." Jake poured the last cup of coffee. "Sorry, I need this more than you," he said as he drained the carafe.

"No problem. I've got some groveling to do, and I don't need the coffee shakes while I'm doing it."

SHANDY HAD PICKED UP a take and bake pizza for dinner on the way home from the dog rescue. "That new bakery could give Alyce some competition," she said. "I wandered in out of curiosity and couldn't resist the pizzas. They had several varieties, and they looked and smelled delicious."

"This meat lovers pizza was great," Justin agreed, with a pat to his flat stomach. "If you bring these home on a regular basis, I'll be in trouble. What else do they sell?"

She wanted to hang her head and scream at the inane question, but it was answer him, or fall to another awkward silence. The meal had been too quiet with Justin and Shandy needing to clear the air in private but needing to keep up a semblance of normalcy in front of Josh.

"Yeah, Mom, get this one again." Josh gathered their plates and took them to the kitchen counter. He turned and faced them with a frown. "But their pies and scones aren't as good as the Welcome Bakery, right?"

She shook her head. "Holmes Baked Bread is different from Alyce's. They specialize in bread, buns, pizza, sausage rolls, that kind of thing. And they sell frozen dough so you can finish baking everything yourself. That way, it's fresh from your own oven."

"Like this take and bake pizza," Josh added. "Cool. But I still want to go to Miss Alyce's bakery, too."

"We will, Josh. Don't worry. Having a second bakery in Welcome will make both the bakers try harder. Competition can be good for businesses."

"But we won't get any competition for our Christmas trees, will we?"

"Maybe not this year, but it could happen next year when other kids see what you've done."

"But they won't have you to help them."

Justin chuckled. "True."

And just like that, the awkwardness of the mealtime vanished. Shandy shared a look with Justin and while the glance promised more private discussion in their immediate future, she felt safer about being honest. He wanted to clear the air as thoroughly as she did.

"Dad, I forgot to tell you about Dilly's new kitten. It's black and white and real cute."

"That's nice, but I hope this isn't a subtle hint for one of your own," he replied with a look at Shandy.

"It's Christmas," Josh said with a hopeful grin.

"A kitten needs more discussion."

"So you two will talk about it, right?"

"We'll see. No promises." She shooed him from the kitchen, releasing him from his nightly clean up chore. "You can have fifteen extra minutes to play your video game."

After an enthusiastic whoop, she was alone with the oaf. They listened as Josh's quick, light footsteps sounded overhead. His bedroom door closed with excited exuberance because he rarely got extra time to play.

"Look, we both jumped to conclusions earlier. Let's call a truce," Shandy said as she loaded the dishwasher without looking at her ex.

"We tried that already. Look how long it lasted."

"I'm not dating anyone," she said, and closed the dishwasher. She turned and leaned against the counter, wanting to see his reaction to her confession. "But I'd like to find someone special. It's time."

He opened his mouth to respond, then closed it again. He nodded and waited a beat before speaking. "I'm sorry I gave you a hard time. It was uncalled for. Once I had time to think, I saw that I was wrong, and that I'd overreacted. You divorced me so you could find someone else. I get it. You wanted to move on. I shouldn't be surprised that you'd be looking."

She tilted her head in surprise. "That's not why I divorced you." How could she explain the mess of feelings she'd been dealing with when she'd filed? "I don't understand why I did it. Maybe it was revenge for you leaving when you did." The words burbled up like a mountain spring, from somewhere deep and cold inside her. "I wanted to hurt you the way you hurt me."

Raw, that's how she felt. Raw then and raw now. If their marriage had failed for lack of interest, or if they'd drifted apart over time, she wouldn't have felt overwhelming anger. Sadness, sure, but not rage.

"Revenge?" Justin's jaw jumped. A sure sign he was trying to stay calm. "I had no choice but to go. I wanted you to come with me. I begged you to move your mom to a facility in Sonoma." He narrowed his eyes as he studied her.

She shook her head against the pain she read in his face. "I couldn't move her. Making a decision like that was too much, too big. The grief was too fresh." It had seared her heart, frozen her mind. "Our lives changed in the space of seconds, and it was all on me. Every decision was life or death." Literally. As an only child everything had landed on her shoulders at once. Her dad had always said he wanted to be an organ donor. She'd honored his wishes in the midst of learning her mother wasn't waking up as expected.

"Moving and the new job," Justin was saying, his eyes stricken. "Your dad and your mom needing life or death decisions." He blew out a breath and his head swung back and forth. "It was too much, and I made it worse."

"We had to back out of our house sale. There were issues with the three laundromats," she recalled the million details that had stolen her sleep, her future, her family. Her dad was dead, and the dawning horror of her mother's coma had cut her in two.

It would be easy to fall back into blaming Justin for leaving. But the truth was, there was nothing here in Welcome but heartache. Maybe she should have moved with him, been free of the laundromats, taken her mom. It didn't matter what bed she was in or what facility. She was never coming back and would never have a life again.

He went to speak but she put up a hand to stop him. "If you'd stayed," she said, "you'd have had no career. No income. The house had been sold at a loss." She chewed her lip because it was her extravagant spending that had put them in the red. She could see it now. So clearly.

"You were thinking of our future," she went on, "and I was stuck in the tornado that had changed everything." She folded her arms across her waist and clutched her elbows, needing to hold on to something or she'd fly apart. The arguments, the tears, the demands, and the ultimatums rose from her heart and swamped her.

"I wasn't noble or unselfish," Justin admitted. "Your parents' needs and then moving you and Josh away from everyone you knew, terrified me. Being jobless terrified me. Not being able to support you terrified me. So, I took the coward's way out and left you to handle the mess. All I had to do was show up for work."

She snorted because Justin the workaholic had used a snide tone to describe his reason for living. But she couldn't let him take all the blame.

"No. You took the job, moved away and your support money allowed me to keep our home after our lawyer got us out of the sale. Your support money gave me breathing room to focus on the laundromats and bring them back to profitable. Without you showing up for work none of that would've been possible."

He shifted where he sat, and she shied away by moving down the counter. She wasn't ready for him to touch, or hug, or kiss her in apology.

"Still, you shouldn't have had to do everything on your own." His gaze was softer than she'd seen it in years. She wasn't sure what that meant, but hers felt softer, too. Forgiving, even. She wanted to roll her shoulders with the lightened feeling.

"Maybe not, but there was no one else." Again, she raised her hands to silence him. "I have to finish this. You were here for Josh, and I've never said how much I needed that. He was the only bright spot in my life and seeing him happy with you was everything, Justin."

"What's going on? Why's Mom crying?" Josh's demand came from the hall. Justin's head turned at the sound. She had no idea how long her son had been there or how much he'd heard. But he'd used a tone that spoke of the man he'd become.

"Josh, I'm not crying," she declared, as she swiped at the moisture on her cheeks. "Not really. Your dad and I are just clearing the air and it felt like smoke got in my eyes. We stirred up some ashes."

"Come here, Buddy." Justin swung his leg out so Josh could sit on his knee as he had as a toddler. But Josh glared at his father, ignored the offer, and came to Shandy.

He threw his arms around her, and she bent to him, but he was tall now and didn't need her to bend. "Are you sure you're okay?" He said softly next to her ear.

"I'm sure. Your father and I are discussing some of the misunderstandings that happened around the time of Grandpa and Gramma's accident. We were too upset at the time to have clearheaded talks about the changes that came after."

"There was a lot of yelling." Josh turn to glare again at his father. "I don't like yelling."

"Nobody does, Buddy. I'm sorry I was loud back then. But I was scared I'd lose you."

His comment made her jerk with surprise. She hadn't considered how frightening it must've been for Justin to trust that he'd see their son when he wanted to. Of course, he'd been scared. Terrified of lots of things, as he'd aptly explained. Now, years later, they'd been objective and open. None of this could've happened without Justin living in the house.

Inside that tornado of change, neither of them had been able to catch their breath and think.

Josh frowned. "But I see you plenty."

"Not enough," Justin said. "We don't see each other as much as we should. I plan to move back to Welcome. We'll see each other all the time." He glanced at Shandy; his eyes hopeful.

The four-bedroom house he'd looked at made her wonder what his real plans for his future were, but she didn't want to open a fresh can of worms when they'd made serious progress talking about the past. When she didn't reply, he looked to Josh.

Josh jerked at the news. "Honest? You're moving back?" He looked up at his mom, his eyes alight.

"That's the plan for the new year. I still have to find a place to live and make more arrangements around a job. I'd appreciate it if you didn't say anything to anyone about my plans yet. The work thing is private family business."

Josh nodded. "Okay. I won't say anything to my friends or at school or anywhere."

"Speaking of family business. We need to discuss these Christmas trees we want to make together. We may have a real business happening here. I have an order from Jake, too."

"Wow! I'm charging Mrs. Bowler twenty bucks each. How much did you ask for?"

Justin and Shandy burst into laughter. "You have no idea what you've started with these trees," she said.

"I want to call your friends and get them to buy from me, too," Josh said, looking at his mother. "I can make lots of money! There's Dilly's parents, and Logan and Elle, and maybe some grandparents, too."

Justin shrugged. "I thought I'd do my best friend a favor, and not charge him. But I played him for a few minutes and asked for fifty bucks." A mischievous grin stole across his handsome face and warmed Shandy's heart. He'd pranked his best buddy and let Josh in on the joke.

"Fifty?! What if he finds out about what I'm charging Mrs. Bowler? And what if she finds out you're not charging Uncle Jake anything at all? Then what'll I do? I can't make some trees for free and others for money. That's not fair."

Shandy laughed. "I'm glad you're thinking this through," she said and turned on the dishwasher.

"I'll abide by whatever you decide," Justin added. "But first we need to outline our expenses. Then we can decide on a fair price."

Shandy wiped the counter and table as they discussed cost of supplies. She allowed a fond smile as she looked at their earnest faces. They had their heads together and Justin was using the calculator on his phone. Josh kept nodding as he listened to his father.

They had nine days to Christmas, and they hoped to deliver their trees on Christmas Eve to everyone who placed an order. They decided that first thing in the morning, Josh would call the adults in their lives to see if he could sell more over the phone. Price? Twenty dollars.

Sooner or later, they'd be asking for her help. "I'll pitch in too, if you need me." They could make it a real Camden family project. Her heart warmed.

Chapter Sixteen

D*ecember 20*
    Shandy hadn't said anything more about the house he wanted, and he'd decided not to push his luck by reminding her of it. With Christmas coming up fast he had no concerns that the place would sell to someone else. If it did sell by some chance, he wouldn't let go of his dream to have a larger home with Shandy, Josh and with luck, more children.

The time with Shandy since their heart-to-heart had been easier than he'd expected. She allowed him to pick up Josh after school and encouraged him to help with cooking dinner because in the last years he'd developed some skills in the kitchen she didn't know about. They occasionally watched movies together as a family. When Josh went to bed, sometimes she stayed on the far end of the sofa until they'd watched their favorite late-night talk show.

The moment the host signed off, Shandy left the room first and never looked back. Sometimes, she responded to his "good night" but other times she didn't. He never pushed.

They'd both said a lot the other day, had brought up old, dangerous emotions and he imagined she was processing everything as much as he was. Justin wasn't used to this much introspection, but one thing had come clear. She understood his position then had been impossible.

She also admitted she'd needed financial stability in order to improve the earning power of the laundromats. Without him leaving and starting his new position, life would have been dire for everyone. Certainly, if he'd stayed, Josh would've suffered through more arguments and like he'd said, he hated yelling.

Not that he'd been right to go. But they both understood that in the end, his move away may have been for the best. As confusing as that seemed, as wrongheaded as it was, as much as it went against everything he understood and wanted from marriage, someone, meaning him, had had to provide for them.

Shandy was smart, dedicated, educated, but working a full-time job when her life had been blown to smithereens wouldn't have worked. She needed the flexibility running the laundromats had given her.

The worst decision they'd made had been getting divorced. If they hadn't, they may have found their way back to each other sooner.

Because despite her leaving him on the sofa every night after watching television, his gut said it was a matter of time before he was back where he belonged. In her bed.

He surreptitiously kept an eye on Josh as his son used his rechargeable screwdriver on the last screw on this five-foot tree frame. "Great job, Buddy. I've got the lights ready to string."

"These frames are painted," Shandy said. "They'll be dry by morning, and we can finish them tomorrow after school." She'd wrapped some in heavy tin foil to make the lights reflect and shine brighter. They were excited to see if the foil gave them the effect she'd been looking for.

"We don't have many more to do," Josh said with a sigh. "Maybe we can deliver some early."

"Sure, we can," Justin said. "We've got so many now that it'll take more than one trip anyway."

Shandy spoke up with pride. "I love that you're donating some to the town. I heard they want to put them on the roof at the Town Hall."

"Yeah," Josh said slowly. "I've been thinking. Maybe we should give some to the food bank too. People can't always pay for Christmas decorations and maybe some families could use them."

Justin cleared his throat as pride rose. "Good idea, Josh."

Shandy's eyes shone in the harsh overhead light of the garage. Wind howled outside as a gale built. Rain splatted against the window in the side door. "We need to call it a night. I've got a pot of homemade soup ready."

"Chicken noodle?" Josh asked with hope in his voice.

"Of course," his mother responded. "It's your favorite."

Shandy placed the lid back on the can of paint she'd been using as Josh left the garage through the interior door. Once in the mudroom he called back to them. "Did you make biscuits, too?"

She laughed and turned to Justin. He stepped close and reached for her hands. He couldn't stop if he tried. Their fingers tangled at her sides and when she didn't pull back, he moved closer.

He'd wanted to kiss her since he'd left her. Three long years. He was working up the courage when he heard her whisper.

"Oh, for pity's sake, just do it."

And suddenly, she pressed her lips to his, lightly at first. Once the shock left him, he deepened the kiss and wrapped her in his arms. One kiss turned into two and soon they were both breathing as if they'd run a mile. His heart raced and lungs tightened.

She sighed against him, softening as her lips opened for more. This kiss was more invitation than affection and he felt the loss when she pulled back. "We have to go inside before he comes looking for us."

He wanted to ask if it would be wrong to have their son see this affection between them, but he couldn't push. He had to follow Shandy's lead. Besides, she turned cold often after a moment of warmth between them. She was hard to read because her feelings were still delicate, but warmer, much warmer.

He pulled back and nodded. "You're right. We have to consider him."

She stood back out of his arms.

"But, Shandy, sometime soon, we'll need to think of us."

She lowered her head so he couldn't read her gaze. "Right. Us." With that, she turned on her heel and left the garage, her back stiff.

But she didn't cut him off at the knees this time, he thought with some hope. He smiled, as the rest of his time here with his family took on a rosy glow.

Half an hour later, content and happy, he sipped at a glass of water at the dinner table. "Your homemade soup and biscuits make a perfect meal after slaving away in the garage." He patted his full stomach. Josh mimicked him.

"Yeah, Dad's right."

Rain slashed the windows and sounded more like pellets than water on the glass. An emergency alert had come in on Shandy's phone about possible power outages and downed trees in the region. Winter in the PNW could bring anything but wildfires. Fires were reserved for drier seasons.

They discussed a movie selection with Josh winning when he mentioned a comedy. "I'm always up for watching a group of kids on bikes save the world."

"Me, too," his wife agreed. "Nothing like plucky teen heroes to warm a mother's heart."

"I'll do the washing up, while you get ready for bed, Buddy." Justin rose and began collecting soup bowls and cutlery. "Your biscuits were great, Shandy. Thanks for making them."

"My pleasure. Since you're being gallant and tidying up the kitchen, I'll slip into the tub for a bit. I need a soak after painting for hours." Shandy arched her back and exaggerated a groan. "Gee, I sound mega old," she said and winked at Josh.

"Yeah, Mom, you're getting creaky."

"I'll creaky you," she growled and gave chase as Josh squealed and raced off down the hall toward his bedroom. Justin heard a few roars and shrieks of laughter as he gathered the dirty dishes. He wanted to keep his mind off his wife relaxing in a tubful of bubbles, but he was only human. Shandy taking a soak had been her signal that she was in the mood.

He overbalanced his stack of bowls at the memory. Luckily, his reflexes were still quick, and he managed not to smash any dishes on the floor. He filled the sink to wash the soup pot and baking sheet.

After Josh's shower, it was Justin's turn. Shandy still hadn't returned to the living area. But the movie was queued and ready to stream as he climbed into the shower/bath combination in the main bathroom. Naturally, Josh had left it steamy. In his new house he'd make sure there were plenty of bathrooms.

As he soaped up, he considered the kiss in the garage. She'd been sweetly welcoming, and something told him he may be sleeping in a real bed tonight instead of the air mattress. He looked forward to sharing the bed with his wife. *Don't overstep. Don't assume that a couple of kisses and a soak in the tub meant the same as it used to.*

But he was a red-blooded man and recognized Shandy's signs. She was as interested as he was. On the cusp of his dreams coming true, he barely noticed that the wind had picked up and rattled the window in the bathroom.

As he dried off, the lights flickered. "Shandy, Josh! You'd better dig out some emergency candles."

A single rap on the bathroom door sounded. "I'm on it already. This doesn't look good," Shandy responded.

When he got to the living room, fresh from the shower, he noticed candles on a table and a camping lantern on the sideboard in front of a large mirror. The reflection would double the light in the room. "You've done this before," he commented with admiration.

She cocked an eyebrow. "Since the fireplace is gas, it'll stay on if we lose power."

His wife was ready for any emergency it seemed. There'd been a time when she'd looked to him for solutions. Things had changed. Shandy was no longer the woman who'd needed him to make everything right. She'd grown a lot because he'd left her to work out her life alone.

He was both proud of her and dismayed at the changes he'd forced on her.

"Let's make popcorn while we can," Josh said as he raced to the kitchen to toss a bag into the microwave.

A few minutes later, they settled in to watch the movie. He sat next to Shandy, with Josh on his other side. He slid his hand to the sofa to find Shandy's, turned palm up. Her fingers twined with his as they sat together enjoying the excitement, adventure, and humor of the world-saving group of young teens.

He glanced at the boy next to him and saw his son enthralled by the story and bravery of the stars. If Josh had noticed the easing of tension between his parents these last few days, he'd given no indication.

But that didn't mean their son wasn't observant. Justin expected to be quizzed at any time. He hoped he had something good to report to him after tonight.

Just as the teens were about to pull the evil creature from the depths of the lake to kill it, the television went dark along with the lights in the house. "Oh no!" Josh wailed. "Right at the best part!"

"They said it was coming, Buddy. Hold on while I get the lantern and candles lit. We can play cards for a while."

Shandy was ahead of him and soon enough the lantern cast a bright glow across the great room. The shadows were long and defined, but they could see well enough. Josh walked to the front door to check on the streetlights. "It's dark out there, too," he reported.

Justin arranged the candles on the dining room table so they could play Crazy Eights while Shandy went to the hall closet to pull out a couple of board games. Their cozy time on the sofa was over for now.

"Let's camp out in front of the fire," Josh suggested. "It'll be warmer and make it fun."

"But—" One sharp look from Shandy cut off Justin's objection. He nodded to accept the inevitable.

"I know," Josh continued. "I can sleep on the sofa and you two can share Dad's airbed. Let's go get it." He jumped up and raced to the den.

Shandy's face crumpled with stifled laughter. "Your face!" she said between quiet gasps. "You look as if your favorite toy fell down a well."

Josh returned with the pillows from Justin's bed. "I need help with the mattress. It's bigger than it looks."

"Your mom and I can get it. But we'll wait a bit to see if the power comes back on." Justin stepped to the dining table and took a seat. "Who's dealing the cards? I vote for Josh."

Chapter Seventeen

Shandy settled Josh on the sofa and then blew out the candles. It didn't seem that the power would be restored anytime soon. She had no choice but to join Justin on his airbed in front of the fireplace. It was the most logical place to sleep. After she turned off the lantern the great room went dark, lit only by the warm glow of the flames.

The air was warm in here, but the bedrooms were chilly. They'd played a couple of rounds of cards, three board games and by then, Josh had seemed ready for bed.

She wasn't sure if she was tired enough to sleep. Tired? No. Wired? Yes. Wired because she'd basically invited Justin into her bed by kissing him, then soaking in a tubful of scented bubbles and then snuggling with him while they watched the movie.

During the game session she and Justin had rubbed feet and toes under the table, a leftover from their early dating days.

She stood frozen, watching as Justin raised the blankets and patted the mattress in invitation. "I won't bite," he said on a husky note.

"But I might," she said silkily. And she wanted to. She wanted to kiss him like a lover, with her lips and tongue and teeth. He'd loved having his earlobes nipped and licked. And she'd loved...

But the smoky light in his eyes told her he was remembering what she'd loved between them, too.

And neither of them could have any of it with Josh sleeping inches away on the sofa.

She dropped her robe to the floor and stepped lightly across the floor to stand over Justin. As she watched, his eyes shifted to their son. When he looked back at her it was with deep regret.

He dropped the blankets and rolled to face the other side of the room, giving her space to crawl in.

She slipped between the sheets, heaved out a big sigh and burrowed her face into the pillow that smelled of Justin. The heat of her husband's body drew her, and she snuggled her back against his.

Long moments passed as she listened to Justin's breathing. It never changed and it would be ages before he slept.

She rose to her elbow and looked over her shoulder at his broad back. "This isn't natural. It doesn't feel right," she whispered.

"I know." He rolled to his back and slid his arm across to her. With a contented sigh, Shandy moved over to lie beside him, settled her head on his shoulder, slid her leg over his and took up their accustomed sleep position. The steady beat of Justin's heart under her ear gave her more comfort than she knew she needed. His heat enveloped her. But one thing was missing, and she waited for it.

Justin dropped a single kiss on her forehead, and all was right in her world.

JUSTIN WOKE IN THE morning spooning a soft, warm Shandy. His hand cupped her full breast under the blankets and his hips were up close and personal with her soft behind. Life was good with Shandy in his arms. Unsure how she'd feel to waken like this, he lifted his hand away and shifted backward to give her room.

She stiffened and he prepared for the Arctic chill his wife had come to wear like a cloak.

But, instead of rising out of the bed and glaring at him, Shandy snuggled back against him and returned his hand to cup her soft flesh in an offering as old as time. He fondled her lightly and leaned over to kiss her ear. She sighed contentedly and then rolled to face him.

"Good morning," she whispered. She touched her lips to his.

He responded in kind, and they shared a smile. "This is some truce we're having."

"Maybe it's more than that. Maybe we should head into peace talks." She bit her lip, looking uncertain.

"I'd like that," he breathed against her temple.

"Me, too. But we'll take this slowly. Rome wasn't built in a day."

His heart wanted to stop right then, to keep from being overrun with hope that could die before the day was out. These weeks with her had been a rollercoaster and one night of snuggling wasn't enough to hang his heart on.

He looked up at the sofa to see his son still fast asleep. "Dibs on the shower," he said. "And the clock on the microwave is flashing. Looks like the power's back on."

"Just in time for breakfast," she said as she rolled off the mattress and rose to her feet. "We'll talk later," she offered with a cocked eyebrow.

"You bet." He had so much to say he wasn't sure where to start. But she'd asked him many times why he was here this month. He'd start with that. The real reason.

An hour later, he dropped his son off at school. Shandy had a meeting set with one of her employees. She was busy until lunch, when he planned to meet her at the bakery. A public place would be less tempting than being at home alone with her. He didn't want their rekindled physical connection to cloud the issues they needed to discuss.

SHANDY'S MEETING ONLY took an hour, and that included the drive. Her employee, Robbie, was a single mom who worked days while her kids were in school. She had ambition and went to community college at night. Her Christmas bonus this year was for Shandy to pay her tuition for the new year. Robbie could have a nicer Christmas with her children if her tuition had already been covered. "Two birds, one stone," Shandy's father used to say.

After a quick visit with her mom, Shandy headed out to the sales office at the new housing project. She wanted to look at the house Justin had mentioned. It was simple curiosity she told herself but knew better. She wanted to figure out what Justin had in mind before they talked things over at lunch.

Logan Hughes met her when she stepped into the trailer on site. After greeting him, she saw the street plan on the wall. Various colored pins stuck out of the map. "These indicate sold or offers in place?"

"The blue means some changes have been requested to floor plans. I like to be aware of that, too."

"I'm interested in seeing the house that Justin saw with you."

"Oh." He sounded doubtful. A cloud passed over his features, turning Logan's usual sunny expression to something darker.

"What? Has Justin lost out to another buyer?"

"No, it's not that. I expected that you'd see it together, that's all."

"Together." It was her turn to sound doubtful. "He didn't ask me to come see it. He told me he liked it. Said it would work for a new family." Four bedrooms? Room for RV parking?

"Shandy. I'm sorry, but you should talk to Justin first." His eyes filled with regret at having to turn down her request.

"You bet I will. We're having lunch today at the bakery."

Logan's shoulders relaxed and he grinned. "Well, then. Give me a call if you decide to come back later. Or, better yet, come see me at the office. And please bring me a cheese scone if you do."

"You got it." But she wasn't leaving here without at least driving by the house. She studied the map for a moment and saw a yellow pin in a corner lot that looked to be two blocks over.

She smiled and waved goodbye to Logan as she drove off.

At the correct corner she saw a two story in a modern style; angular with a steep-pitched roof, covered by corrugated steel. River rock columns on the veranda took away from the stark, industrial look and gave the front of the house an inviting appeal. As she turned the corner, she saw the extra driveway that Justin liked. It was more of a parking pad that stretched from the sidewalk to the far side of the lot. But the backyard was still big enough for a family to enjoy.

She flashed on the image of a group barbecue with kids using a trampoline in the corner. A climbing rose arbor could camouflage whatever big thing sat on the gravel pad.

"An RV? Or a boat? What's happened to the workaholic I used to know?" she asked the empty car. Funny, she didn't get an answer, but she'd be certain to ask Justin when they had lunch together. No way would he take weekends away if he owned a vineyard. He'd be buried in work.

But the vineyard was only three miles away. He'd have a short commute.

She'd have to leave now if she wanted to be on time for lunch. She did a U-turn and headed toward town.

Snuggling with Justin through the night had felt fabulous and right. She hadn't slept that well since he'd left. Back then, as angry as they'd been, she'd still rested her head on his chest to sleep. There was something about hearing him breathe and being close to his heat that eased her.

That much hadn't changed, she mused. But they were different people now. So much had happened in the last three years. Josh had gone from a little boy to a big one. She'd learned about business and apparently, Justin had learned a few things about himself.

Aside from Josh growing, none of the other things would've happened if their lives hadn't been torn apart. She'd still be the dutiful wife to a career-obsessed husband. Her dad would've closed the laundromats and retired. They'd have moved to California to be closer to her, Justin, and Josh. But that's not what happened.

Life had happened and a bad thing had happened to good people. Circumstances had shifted their worlds and had forced her and Justin to change.

Was it enough to learn from? Could they move forward from here? In peace?

She held a lot of residual anger. It wasn't pretty and it didn't make her feel proud when she let it get the better of her. She had to find a way to let it go. Being a bitter, angry woman held no appeal and ultimately, a dark, dreary future.

Parking was at a premium as she slowly rolled along Main looking for a spot. The downtown shopping area was lively and revived since the town had banned national chains from opening on Main Street. The shops and restaurants were local owners with their unique styles and menus. Downtown Welcome was a popular place for shoppers who wanted something different.

She ended up parking close to Clay's veterinary clinic at the far end, which sat kitty corner to the new bakery. People stood outside staring through the window and pointing at the displays. She already seen that there were no pies or cakes in the window. Holmes Baked Bread specialized in savory breads and buns, not sweets.

She turned for her stroll along the block to the Welcome Bakery and realized as she waved or called greetings to several people, whom she'd known all her life, that she loved this town.

Those same people had eventually stopped asking how her mom was. They understood that they'd hear when Brenda was gone. They would come to her mom's service and share their stories of her mom and her dad. Some of them would say that the end had given Brenda peace.

Shandy would agree.

As she approached the bakery, Candace stepped out wearing a frown that marred her usual sunny expression.

"Hi! What's got you looking worried?" She stopped in front of the window where the stools were taken by diners, giving her and Candace an unintended audience. Shandy stepped to the far side of the sidewalk and waved her friend closer.

"Oh, Shandy. Hi." Candace bit her lip and joined her. Then she glanced around to see if anyone was within earshot. "It's that bakery up the block. Everyone's talking about how good it is. I'm worried for my mom, but she seems blind to it."

Guilt trickled along Shandy's nerve endings. Suddenly the pizza they had the night before seemed disloyal. "I hear they focus on bread and buns," she replied to assuage her guilt. "Does that take business away from Alyce?"

"They sell sausage rolls that compete with some of our savory scones and things." Candace jutted her chin. "I don't like it. Next thing he'll be entering cake contests or the county fair next summer. What if he makes really good pie and he plans to spring it on us out of the blue?"

"He doesn't. From what I hear bakers often specialize. Have you been inside yet?"

"No. Of course not. I'll never set foot in there."

Shandy nodded. "Never say never. I have no idea what he looks likes. Word is he spends most of his time in the back. A bit anti-social if you ask me. You could go in, ask for him, and then use your best smile to get some info."

"Spy?"

Shandy shrugged. "You think he didn't take a good look at your mom's operation before deciding to settle here?"

"Mom told me he's returned to Welcome from somewhere in Europe. He was vague about *where* in Europe."

"Obviously somewhere that makes great bread and pizza. Italy, maybe?"

"I didn't mention pizza. Have you been inside?"

Shandy drew in a deep breath and let it out slowly. "Don't be disappointed, but we've already had his take and bake." Her mouth watered remembering the flavor of the toppings and the lightness of the dough. *Perfection*.

"Hmph. Maybe I should do some reconnoitering." Candace frowned, considering her options. "Mom said he talked to her before dawn a couple of months ago. He gave her a start because his hoodie was up, and he stepped out of the shadows. Very cloak and dagger."

"That's mysterious. But bakers start work early. It makes sense he'd show up in the dark. He was guaranteed to catch her." Shandy wondered about the hidden face, but maybe it was a cold morning and he'd been waiting a while.

"I guess, but she didn't get a good look at his face. I find that a bit strange."

"I only saw a teenager at the counter when I was inside. But then, I was busy looking at everything but the people." She hadn't been the only customer either, but Candace didn't need to hear that.

Her friend sighed. "Maybe I should do the same thing he did to Mom. Show up before dawn with a sneak attack. Maybe the surprise would loosen his tongue."

"If you do go in the wee hours, bring Dayna over to spend the night with us. She knows Josh well and she'd be happy to come over."

"That seems like a lot of hassle, but I can't wake Dayna and then leave her in the car while I ambush the man. Knowing Dayna, she'd jump out of the car and come looking for me."

"She's a very self-sufficient child. But my offer holds if you want to try the early morning meeting."

The other woman shook her head. "I'd rather be around other people if I begin a conversation with the man. But thanks for the offer.

I'll let you know what I decide." Candace rolled her eyes. "If I do anything at all. My father says I should leave it to Mom."

"He's probably right. Maybe you're not cut out for spying," Shandy replied and raised her brow. "But I'm sure you remember how to flirt. You could go in, ask for the owner and then turn on the charm."

Candace snorted. "I'm rusty. Like, really rusty."

"Or you could just let it go. If your mom's not worried, then she's probably up for the challenge of a little competition. She knows best." Alyce Markham was a savvy businesswoman, and, like Mr. Markham, Shandy felt certain the bakery would survive.

"It better not become a *lot* of competition, or this man will have me to answer to." With that, Candace stalked off. Shandy watched her go, wondering how their first meeting would play out. *Oh, to be a fly on the wall.*

But right now, she needed to focus on Justin and have an honest heart-to-heart. Being in public should make it easier for her to contain her always-bubbling resentment.

Butterflies fluttered through her as she smoothed her puffy jacket and stamped some clinging snow off her boots as she waited for a young family to exit the doorway to the bakery. The chatter inside the toasty warm shop seemed to be mostly about the power outage from the windstorm.

Alyce was busy assuring everyone that the power had been on in time for her to bake the day's special orders this morning. "Four a.m. I'm here. Rain or shine or windstorm," she called to a table full of regulars.

She graced Shandy with a broad, welcoming smile. "Your man's in the back booth, waiting."

It was on the tip of her tongue to say Justin wasn't her man, but instead, she gave the friendly baker a salute and strolled toward the last booth, where he sat, looking nervous. That was the thing with relationships that stretched back years, you could read a person's mood from yards away.

Justin tapped a finger on his long thigh and watched her approach. As she slid into the banquette across from him, he spoke. "I'm glad you're here. I wasn't sure you'd come."

"Neither was I," she admitted. "But I'm here and there's no Josh to get in the way of our conversation." And it was public. She'd keep her voice modulated, cool, and calm.

"I want to talk with you about so many things. But we need to not get angry." He nudged a cappuccino in her direction. He'd ordered for her, which used to be typical. She'd taken a lot for granted with Justin.

She smiled her thanks and took a sip. "May I start?"

He nodded, but his tension was palpable. She needed to ease his mind so he could listen to her words.

"First of all, I'm not dating. Sure, I've had a couple of dates since you left, but nothing that led anywhere." Maybe she'd gone out with men who she knew were safe. That she wasn't all that attracted to. Her fleeting desire to rekindle a years-old crush had been a master class in failure. Thank God, they'd become friends since.

She and Clay shared a mutual love of Mercy and after a few months she'd been grace personified about Shandy. One day, she'd tell Justin about it. Especially the part about how neither of them wanted things to move forward. She'd had her mind on Justin and his heart belonged to Mercy, although Shandy suspected Clay had been fighting it.

"I'm sorry I jumped on you about dating." Justin flushed deep red. "Even if you were seeing someone, it's not my business." He bit his lip as if he'd like to say more.

She appreciated that he didn't. "What if I said it could *be* your business?"

His face broke. His eyebrows winged up, his mouth lifted, his eyes brightened as her words sunk in. "Could be?"

"I've been wondering why you wormed your way into my house." There were no bed bugs in the local hotels. "By the time I checked on that reported bed bug infestation, Josh was already thrilled with having you here."

He raised in hands in surrender and tossed his best friend under the bus in one sentence. "That was Jake's idea."

"I'm sure it was," she said with a soft smile. "Anyway, I've come to see the truth of why you've come back. The vineyard, the family time, even building the Christmas tree frames was to show me what we lost."

"Did it work?"

Her heart squeezed as she watched him squirm. "Of course it did. I've known for a long time that I'd demanded our divorce because I was angry. But the question is, what was I angry about?"

He blinked and she suspected she saw a sheen of tears, but then it was gone. He shook his head. "I didn't want to leave you like that," he murmured. "At the time, I didn't see any other way to keep us together. You wouldn't move and I don't blame you for that."

"But you did blame me."

"Maybe, a little, at the time. I was an ass to push you when you needed me to stand still and be here for you. But I was terrified of losing my job. My dad was never a provider. I couldn't be him. I couldn't fail the way he did."

"I know *now*." If she hadn't been blinded by grief and worry, she'd have understood at the time. "But I wasn't angry with you so much as angry with the world, my dad for dying the way he did, for his death injuring my mother. Our lives changed in an instant and I couldn't cope. But I had to keep putting one foot in front of the other while I dealt with my mom's condition."

Josh had been young and didn't understand the accident or his grandpa's sudden death and the strange way he'd also lost his gramma. She was alive, but not living a life, and to a seven-year-old it made no sense. He talked about her sleeping and waking up. Shandy had wanted to scream at him to stop assuming his gramma was coming back to them. The agony of those conversations still made her break out into a sweat.

Justin went to speak and reached to clasp her hand where it sat on the tabletop. She pulled back and shook her head. "I have to finish."

"Okay." He looked scared. Not even then, when they'd been at their worst, had Justin looked scared.

"I want to go to counselling." She pulled in a deep draft of air. Let it seep out again. "I believe now that I need to let go of a lot of stuff; anger, maybe resentment, maybe grief, I don't know, but if we're going to move forward,"—she waved a hand back and forth between them— "I need to talk to someone who can help me." Brianna had offered the name of a good counsellor and Shandy planned to book an appointment.

Justin's eyes widened as he took in what she'd said. He nodded and sagged like a worn-out pillow. "I'll come with you if you want," he said. "I'll do anything to fix this. Marrying you and having Josh were the smartest things I ever did. There's never been anyone but you for me."

"I know," she responded softly. "It's the same for me." Her voice hollowed. "From the moment we met out at the lake, I understood you'd be important to me." She hadn't realized at the time that she was looking at her future when she saw his hazel eyes light up at the sight of her. He'd driven her home and hadn't even kissed her when he parked in front of the house. So, she'd leaned over and brushed his cheek with her lips. She'd asked if she'd see him the next day and he'd grinned his honey-sweet smile and said, "Always."

Love had come to them at the same time and from that night forward they'd been together constantly. Between school, and working two part-time jobs, he'd become a fixture in her parents' home, to the point where her mom had purchased some of his favorite food. She'd been unaware of his parents' financial straits until much later. There had been days back then when the only meal Justin got was one Brenda prepared. Most months, he'd had to contribute to the rent at home.

Of course, after a childhood of want, the adult Justin couldn't be unemployed or broke. He was driven to provide well. Her father had admired Justin's ambition while her mother had seen the love in his eyes for Shandy.

"You lovebirds in the back. Food's up!" Alyce called.

Chapter Eighteen

Justin heard the call from Alyce that their food was ready and hopped up to get their order from the counter. Shandy liked the soup and half-sandwich special for lunch while he went for a full sandwich on a long roll. The bread here was the best he'd ever had. When he slid back into the booth after depositing the tray he spoke. "I grab a loaf of bread and a bunch of rolls to freeze when I'm heading home. There's nothing as good as Alyce's bread anywhere else. Hand to God."

For a few moments they busied themselves getting their plates and cutlery situated. Shandy could barely look him in the eye. "That new bakery where I got the pizza specializes in bread. That's why the crust was crazy delicious." She kept her voice low and soft. "Candace is upset about the place being down the block, but she says Alyce is okay with it."

"Oh, yeah? I'll keep with my routine. The pizza was great, but Alyce's bread is the best. When I find something I like, I stick with it." He looked at her hopefully and she was certain he'd moved away from the topic of buns and bread.

When she picked up her soup spoon, he slid his hand over hers. "I hate that you're taking the blame here. It feels as if you believe you're the only one who acted out of anger. Maybe even the only one who needs to talk to someone who can help."

She froze, her eyes wide and anxious.

"I love you, Shandy. I always have. But I haven't always treated you that way. I'm sorry, so sorry for storming off like a kid whose favorite toy broke."

She swallowed hard and a single tear lay track down her cheek. He groaned. "Oh, honey. That's not the first tear you shed because of me. I'm ashamed of myself for bringing you to tears when you were already crying for your mom and dad."

"No, it's not that. I'm relieved that you're seeing things from my side. You've never looked there before."

He swallowed hard. His confession was long overdue, but God, it felt good. "I haven't. To be honest, I tried hard not to see your side, because if I did, I'd have seen myself for the jerk I was being." *What a mess!*

He forked up some coleslaw, but held his fork in the air, waiting.

Shandy gave him a slow, indulgent smile. The same smile she gave Josh when he apologized for being a normal, rambunctious kid.

"But to be fair," she said after she chewed a bite of sandwich, "I've ignored what you were going through, too. You took providing for us seriously. Budgeting, investments, and bonuses were uppermost in your mind most days. I believed it was the work that you put ahead of me and Josh, but that wasn't exactly right, was it?"

"Maybe not." He sighed and let his mind go back to hard times he usually tried not to remember. "My parents struggled because my father wanted his luck to change rather than to work toward stability. Things were supposed to magically turn around for them." He shook his head with the memories. From an early age, he'd known that he'd have to help out.

"Meanwhile, my sisters and I were contributing to the rent from our paper routes." Before they were old enough to deliver papers, there were nights they'd gone to bed hungry. Not often, but enough that he and his sisters remembered sharing the last of the bread. They'd wait to eat until just before bed, hoping to be asleep before the hunger came back. "I just figured out why I stock up on buns from here before I leave for my place."

It was her turn to cover his fingers with a comforting hand. "I'm sorry I forgot about how you suffered as a kid. I should have remembered. I was in a fog after the accident and when my dad died. The only emotion that broke through that fog was my rage at the world. Most of it landed on you."

He made a show of brushing off his shoulders and she smiled at his antics.

They focused on their food for a few minutes. Shandy's broken eyes cleared, and he set aside his darker memories.

"How are your parents doing?" she asked. "I'm sorry I haven't asked until now."

"Mom calls to tell me when another scheme has disappointed them. I send money to cover their rent while my sisters send gift cards for the grocery store chain mom likes. It's not wise to send them cash because they'll run to the track to bet on a sure thing." He never knew if his mom told their father how she paid for the food.

Most people in Welcome assumed the elder Camdens had retired to San Diego, but another get-rich-quick scheme had lured them there. But rent, even in a trailer, was too high for them some months.

"What will you do when they can't manage?"

"We'll help them more. Probably move them closer to one of us." Soon he and his sisters would have to help in a significant way. But that was a problem for another day.

Today, he wanted to reconnect with his wife. His Shandy.

"THIS FEELS GOOD, THIS talking," Shandy said after finishing her cappuccino and lunch. "A real conversation for a change. I'd like to continue over a piece of chocolate cake."

"Sure thing. I'll be right back with it. And a piece of pie for me."

It was too soon to leave this public place. In the bakery, there were parameters to what they said. Besides, it was calming to breathe in the scents, to smell the warm yeasty bread. The hominess was a balm they seemed to need. Being alone with Jake before touching on a few more topics would be a mistake.

Shandy felt lighter than she had in too long. Hopeful, too. Dare she hope they could have a chance? He claimed he still loved her and her love for him simmered under the anger and hurt. He'd seemed genuinely interested in counselling and that was a great start.

She smiled when he returned with another tray. She slid his lemon meringue pie to his side of the table and took her plate of cake while he stacked the new tray with the previous one.

He reddened. "Can we talk about the house I saw?"

She nodded happily. The topic was lighter and included a look at the future, not rehashing the past. "I just came from there. I put Logan on the spot by wanting to see it and he said I should ask you about it. So, is that where you see yourself when you start at the vineyard? It's a short commute, but I still can't imagine you with an RV." Then the light dawned. "Unless you see your parents living in it?"

"No!" He looked shocked. "Not at all. I don't want to get ahead of myself, but I like to think of us living in there. With more children." He put up a hand to stop her speaking. "Josh is good with young kids, maybe he'd like to be a big brother?"

The hope that sprang from his eyes made Shandy smile back, but she couldn't agree so quickly. Could she? A larger family was what she'd wanted. Still wanted. "I'm sure he'd love to have a sister or brother, but I'm not sure this is the time to discuss it."

"Or one of each?" Justin's enthusiasm had him talking over her. "That house has enough room and the second and third would have each other when Josh goes to college."

Shandy fell back against the banquette in shock. "You've put a lot of thought into this. How long have you been planning for a bigger family?"

"Since last Christmas," he admitted. "Actually, always. I kept letting work interfere with our family decisions." He smiled into her eyes and made her belly flutter in a familiar way. "But, like I said, we shouldn't get ahead of ourselves."

"Right. We shouldn't." Maybe discussing it now *was* the right time. At least she'd know what was in his heart. She took a mouthful of cake and pondered while she chewed and swallowed. "But we're in this together now. It's not just you or me talking about ourselves. These are big plans you're asking about. Life-changing plans."

"You're right, but I've never wanted anything more in my life. Not even the first time I proposed, because I was certain you wanted to marry me. Now, I'm a wreck. We've got a long way to climb out of the hole we've dug."

"A long way," she echoed. But she could see the light. "I love you, too."

His shoulders slumped and his eyes went moist. He jabbed his thumbs into them to stem the tears.

She reached both hands toward his and they entwined their fingers. The warmth from his hands and the heat of his gaze set her heart racing. "Let's spend the rest of this Christmas season remembering what we had and forget about how we let it slip away."

"Deal." He sniffed and the love in his gaze burned his initials into her heart.

"There's still time before school's out. We could go look at the house together." Her tone was nonchalant, but she couldn't keep her happiness out of her eyes. He responded with a wide grin.

"Let's take both vehicles. I want to try out the garage. Logan says there's room in there for a workbench, but I've got my doubts." He gave her a broad smile. "I want to do more projects with Josh, so we'll need room to work."

"I don't want to get your hopes up," she cautioned. "I'm not sure I want to move or how things will be after we go for counselling."

He nodded with two quick dips of his head. "You're right. We might not like the place. And the counselling could bring up a lot of resentment." His eyes shadowed. "We'll clear the air though and come out the other side. I'm sure of it."

"I'm cautiously optimistic."

"I'll take it."

She followed him back to Logan's sales office and they walked into the building together.

Logan's smile lit his whole face at first sight. He rose from behind his desk and strode toward them, hands outstretched to shake. "Glad to see you here together. This bodes well, right?" His eyes danced from hers to Justin's and back again.

"We're willing to look. Justin hasn't convinced me of anything yet." But, oh, she wanted him to. She wanted this heady feeling of joy to be the main emotion of her day. Today and every day. Justin reached for her hand as she reached for his. Their fingers tangled and held and warmed.

The same way her heart did. Logan gave them the key and his promise to keep the sales pitch to a minimum as they walked out of the office.

Justin wanted Shandy to love the house as much as he did. Not just because it was practical and roomy, but because buying it meant they were letting go of the past and starting fresh. Logan had given him the remote control for the garage door opener, and he used it. He parked inside the garage and walked back out to wave Shandy in.

Shandy climbed out, swinging her car door wide open. "Logan wasn't kidding, this garage seems extra wide."

"It's a triple with a double door. The original purchaser ordered it this way, but it means we get lots of room for storage and a work area. We could put an extra fridge or freezer out here, too." He couldn't get the idea of a larger family out of his head. He watched as she scanned the interior.

She nodded her agreement and came to stand with him. "I see why you like it. And I can see you and Josh working out here together. You've been having a ton of fun building the Christmas trees."

She walked down the drive only to turn and survey the house from the sidewalk. "I love the veranda. The corrugated roof is different and looks industrial, but still, the façade of the house is classic now that I take more time to look."

"Wait until you see the kitchen. In the years I've lived alone, I've been cooking more. I appreciate the features this place has now, like the water faucet at the stovetop for filling large pots. No more lifting from the sink in the island."

She made an appreciative noise and let him hold her hand as they unlocked the door and entered. Kicking off their snowy boots, they walked on sock-covered feet through the main floor. As they passed through the great room she spoke. "I'm blown away by the finishes," she said as she indicated the modern look of the floor to ceiling fireplace that stretched to the second story ceiling.

The house had industrial touches throughout but was warmed by the color choices on the walls. Golden white in the living areas gave way to buttery yellow in the kitchen.

"Look up," he said and pointed to the ceiling where a large light tube brought brighter-than-daylight sunshine into the room. "It's this bright because the tube lining is highly reflective. The light seems brighter as it enters the kitchen. We won't need the lights on even on a cloudy day."

She seemed suitably impressed and wandered the rest of the kitchen, opening and closing drawers and cabinets. She spun to face him. "I love it, but you knew I would."

"Sue me for knowing you so well."

She stepped into his arms, and he held her, his wife, his love. "I don't want to push you into anything, but do you want to see the rest of the place?" They had work to do to keep their family together, but from the look in her eyes, she was onboard.

"Yes."

That was all she said and all he needed to hear. After that, it was a whirl of room inspections. At a landing halfway up the stairs was a doorway to a room over the garage. "This space is huge," she muttered.

"There's a four-piece bath over there, the fireplace is in the corner so as not to dominate the space and there's room to partition off a small bedroom. In case your mom can ever come home."

She gasped. "Justin, this is incredibly thoughtful. Truly considerate."

"Can't put her in the basement and the upper floor will be noisy with more children. We can put in one of those seats that goes up the stairs for her if she needs it."

She blinked and he worried she might cry, but she rallied. "Or this would make a wonderful games room with a pool table or a craft table. Or both."

"If she never comes home, then yes, we'll have the room here for whatever works for us and our family."

She spun away then and strode up to the upper floor. Three smaller bedrooms had ample space for children and the larger suite for them was perfectly set up with an ensuite with a walk-in steam shower, a soaker tub, two sinks, and a water closet that included a bidet. "This is an amazing bathroom," she said. "In fact, the house is wonderful. There's only one problem."

"Only one? With our track record, that's hard to believe," he quipped, happier with her approval than he probably should be. It wasn't wise to expect Shandy to remain happy for long.

"Who's cleaning four bathrooms? As it is now, I'm swamped with getting Josh everywhere he needs to be, covering for the odd shift at a location, and keeping our smaller home clean."

"We'll hire a house cleaner. Or a nanny slash housekeeper to live in when we need to."

"And where will they stay?"

He could tell by her tone that she was still happy, still feeling positive and his heart swelled. "We'll build a suite in the basement."

"You've thought of everything," she murmured and stepped close enough to kiss.

So he did. Shandy flowed into his arms and kissed him back. He held her close and smoothed his hand down her back to cup her bottom. She sighed and opened her mouth to deepen the kiss.

He groaned, lost in possibilities.

Chapter Nineteen

*C*hristmas Eve – *The Mall*

"Okay, we've looked at a dozen different gift baskets for your mom's favorite body lotion and creams," Justin said to Josh. "This one comes with one of those scrubby things she likes. And it's pink."

"But this one has a purse with it. She'd like that, right?"

"It's called a toiletries bag for when she travels. She can take this stuff along." This decision had taken longer than Justin had anticipated. But Josh had more money than the twenty-five dollars he'd started with before they'd built and sold the Christmas tree frames. "How about we buy her the one with the bag and also, a package of the scrubby things."

His son's face lit up at the suggestion. "Yeah! Except Mom never goes anywhere but to work." He picked out both gifts and smiled happily. He tossed them into the hand basket. "Now, I gotta find something nice for Dilly."

Justin checked the time on his phone. "Your mom's waiting for us. We shouldn't have left this to the last minute." He'd fallen into an old habit by putting off his Christmas shopping until the day before Christmas. Shandy would notice for sure, but since their talk at the bakery, Justin had been caught in meetings with his new partners in the vineyard and touring the place with Sven. There was a lot to do before he took over the reins and he'd put all that ahead of this shopping trip.

Guilt wormed its way through his gut. Here he was, teaching his son to let his family responsibilities slide because business came first. They'd finished the last tree this morning and delivered it on the way to the mall. But Josh was antsy about finding another gift. "Dilly? That's Clay and Mercy's girl, right?" He recalled the way Josh had taken her in hand on the night of the tree lighting downtown. They'd been close as mourning doves with their heads together, sharing the sights and lots of giggles. And he'd kissed her cheek when the lights came on.

"Yeah, Dilly's my friend and she likes coloring. I want to get her a book and a pack of markers. The kind that wash off in case she colors outside the lines and marks up her dad's table."

"You've put some thought into this."

"Yep," he replied and headed off toward the toy section. Justin felt like a barge behind a tugboat, but he was proud of his son for thinking of the little girl. He called Shandy and explained about this last-minute gift and why they'd be later than expected.

"That's cute," she said, happily. "I'm sure they'll be friends for life. They're quite attached."

"What are you up to?"

"Wrapping presents. You don't need to rush home. I left this to the last minute and I'm panicking."

"You have no idea how glad I am to hear you say that." He chuckled. "I'll explain why when I get you alone." He wove his way through other men who stood like sentinels as they stared at ladies' robes and slippers. To a man, they had eyes glazed over by indecision. "Hey, guys, buy the pink ones," he joked as he strode past. "Sorry, Shandy, you wouldn't believe how many men are here for last-minute gifts."

She released an unladylike guffaw that made him chuckle. "Yeah, I know. I'm here, too," he confessed. "But at least I feel guilty about it."

"Did you mention us having another heart-to-heart? I'll meet you at the fireplace at ten." He could hear joy in her voice. They'd been doing this lately: planning their talks, being open, which made the chains of remorse dribble away with each conversation. He was still sleeping in the den, but things were definitely looking up. Shandy hadn't been angry or resentful for days. At least, not that she'd shown.

Josh took a left into another aisle, and he followed. "It's a date," Justin said into the phone. "And soon, we'll have a real one."

"I'm looking forward to it." She ended the call, but he heard her chuckling as she tapped the phone.

He had plans for New Year's Eve if his Christmas worked out the way he hoped it would. But first, he had to get his son out of this store, get home, wrap their gifts for Shandy and now, Dilly, and head out for a Christmas Eve get together with friends.

The good thing about hanging with other parents with young children was that it was an early evening. There by five, home again by eight. Early bedtime was a godsend on Christmas Eve.

BY FIVE-FIFTEEN, AT Mercy and Clay's home, all the children were grouped around the babies on the great room floor. Each child waited excitedly for their one present to open on Christmas Eve. Dilly sat beside her baby sister Autumn. Liam and Jorja, Elle's twins held their younger twin brother and sister, while her oldest, Daniel, looked on. Josh mimicked Daniel's attempt at a fifteen-year-old's maturity and sophistication and feigned looking unmoved by the younger children's obvious excitement.

Looking around the room at the group of adults she'd come to love like family, Shandy was a dazed by all that had happened in the last couple of years. First loves had returned, a movie career had taken off, a stalker had been exposed, a nice guy had won the girl and her beautiful children. And, in the most amazing twist of all, her husband had returned a changed man.

Their future was bright and starting in the new year, she and Justin would begin the counselling process. Was she a tad scared? Yes. Would she do it anyway? Absolutely.

What she and Justin had once was worth the work. What they stood to gain was everything she wanted. Tonight, she'd show him all the ways she loved him.

He strolled over with a drink in each hand. "Punch, lightly spiced with rum."

"Perfect," she said, "everything's perfect."

Clay and Mercy clapped their hands to get everyone's attention. The children hushed and their eyes went wide with hopeful expectation. "Daniel, being the oldest, will be our Santa's helper tonight. Each child gets one surprise gift to open."

Daniel rose and made sure to name each child clearly, including the babies. As the gifts were handed out and the wrapping was torn and tossed around the room, the noise level in the great room rose to the two-story ceiling.

The adults retreated to the kitchen to allow the children to enjoy their gifts. They stood together in a circle. "To us!" The toast went up simultaneously.

Jake held Brianna's hand as he raised his other one for silence. "We have an announcement. We may have to rent a hall for this party next year, because there may not be room for the baby we're having." Brianna snuggled into Jake's side as another cheer went up. She sipped at a flute of orange juice.

Karen and her fiancé, Duncan, cheered the loudest. "I'm going to be a grandmother!" Karen squealed and burst into happy tears. The other grandparents in the group rallied around the happy, older couple.

"Wow. Imagine Jake being a dad," Justin said into Shandy's ear. "When for years he shut everyone out of his life."

"It's time," Shandy said, feeling a deep warmth and happiness for her friends. "He and Brianna deserve every joy." She stretched up to his ear. "And so do we. When we go home tonight, you can let the air out of that air mattress. You won't be needing it anymore."

AN HOUR LATER JUSTIN tucked his son into bed. "You need to get to sleep, or Santa won't come."

"I'm ten, Dad, not three."

"Still, your mother and I want you to get a good night's sleep. We have a long day tomorrow."

"Okay. Uh, can I ask you something?" Josh's eyes picked up the glow from the hall light. He looked curious but happy. Happier than normal.

"Shoot. I'm listening."

"Are you and mom kissing and stuff? Because it's okay with me if you are." The last came out on a rush of breath.

In their many discussions, Justin hadn't considered that his son might want to offer an opinion or approval. Or a veto. Shandy hadn't mentioned it, either. But he had to say something. "I take it you've noticed a change between us."

"Yeah, I guess. I don't know, it's like the house is brighter or...something." He didn't have the words to explain the difference the last few days had brought. Justin wasn't convinced he had the right words, either.

He scrubbed his chin, searching for the best way to say this. "Remember when the power went out and we had to sleep in the living room by the fireplace?"

"That was fun."

"Your mom and I remembered how much better we sleep when we're together." Nothing had happened but some cuddling, but if Justin had to bet on it, that night had been the beginning of a reconciliation attempt. He was still uncertain about the future because there was a long way to go emotionally. He had faith that counselling would help, but that still wasn't a guarantee.

"If you're moving into the bedroom with her, that's great," Josh announced. "People who have children should sleep together. That's why their beds are big."

Justin chuckled. "The sooner you roll over and go to sleep the sooner I can get out of here and flatten that airbed."

"Does this mean you're moving back home?"

"It means your mom and I are going to try really hard to be happy again."

Josh spoke in a hushed whisper. "Then I've got my Christmas wish already."

"I believe I have mine, too." He bussed his son's forehead and wished him good night. When he turned toward the doorway, Shandy stood watching them. She held out her hand and he took it.

The airbed could wait. Right now, the light in his wife's eyes called to him. All he wanted; all he'd ever dreamed of waited for him.

IN THE MORNING, JOSH tapped on the bedroom door three times and then called in. "Mom, Dad, it's time to get up. It's Christmas!"

Shandy heard her son and snuggled backward into the furnace of her husband's embrace. She clasped his hand where it rested over her breast and squeezed lightly. "Are you awake?" she whispered.

"How could I not be?" Justin groaned and leaned over her to kiss her cheek. She turned her head to let him capture her mouth. "Thank you," he murmured. "I love you."

"I love you," she responded.

"We'll make this work," he promised.

"I know." She already felt more connected to Justin than she had before their divorce. Sure, they had things to talk about, but following the lead of a counsellor should help them dig out the remaining bits of disappointment and regret. Life was coming right again, and she'd do whatever it took to keep their world turning as it should. "Josh, come on in and say good morning," she called to their son.

The bedroom door opened slowly, and his excited face leaned into the room. "Hi, Mom, hi, Dad. Are you two getting up soon?" He sidled in and walked cautiously toward the bed.

She sat up with her back against the headboard and Justin followed suit. She held out her arms and grinned. "Merry Christmas," she said as her boy fell into her arms and hugged her hard.

"Merry Christmas, Mom."

His hugs were precious now. As he'd gotten older, he'd become less inclined to public displays of affection, but apparently this counted as a big day, because Josh ran around to the other side of the bed and hugged his father, too. Shandy felt the prickle of threatening tears and patted her eyes with her fingertips.

"Come on down soon. I checked the coffee, and nobody remembered to set the timer. I'm not sure how to make it."

Justin made a shocked face. "What? No coffee on Christmas morning?"

Josh laughed and jumped up and down. "Hurry UP!"

Shandy rose and pulled her robe on over her nightie, shuffled into her slippers, and tossed her pillow at her husband. "Since you forgot to set up the coffeemaker last night, you have to do it now. Fair's fair."

He cocked an eyebrow and chuckled. "Fine, blame me for forgetting."

The look they shared could burn the sheets, but they managed to get themselves into the kitchen while Josh ran to the Christmas tree. Gifts and packages spread out from under the tree.

In a flurry, he picked up boxes and bags to read gift tags.

"Here's one for Mom," he called. "It's from me," he said proudly and held up a bag with Santa's picture splashed across the front. He hurried to where she leaned on the counter waiting for Justin to finish with the coffeemaker.

"Open it," Josh demanded.

She mugged a tired face. "Without my first coffee?"

"Yes." His dear face looked so excited she laughed.

"The coffee will be ready in no time. Let's go sit and you can open this fabulous gift," Justin suggested, with a tousle of Josh's hair.

They trooped into the great room and took their seats. Josh handed Shandy the bag and she made a show of inspecting the picture. "Wait, did you black out Santa's teeth?" The Jolly Elf grinned a gap-toothed smile.

Her two favorite men howled with laughter. "Dad made me do it!"

"I didn't! It was his idea, I swear."

She gave them her stern mom face but couldn't hold it for more than a second. She pulled the pretty tissue paper out of the bag and set it aside, while Josh vibrated with excitement. The first thing she found was a package of her favorite bath sponges. "I love these," she said with a smile for her boy. "And what's this?" She pulled out a wicker basket filled with her favorite body lotion and body wash. There were full-sized versions and travel-sized bottles as well. "And look, there's a travel case too."

"I'll be back with coffee for you," Justin said to Shandy. "Josh, it's your turn to open a gift. That blue one looks good," he hinted.

JUSTIN POURED TWO MUGS of fresh brew and drew in a deep breath. He'd made it to Christmas Day without being kicked out of the house. Last night had cemented his place with Shandy. Their doubts had fled as they'd shared themselves. Hard-pressed not to crow like a rooster, he slipped a hand into his robe pocket and fingered the velvet-covered box he'd hidden there.

From the great room, he heard Shandy thank Josh for her awesome gift. Josh recounted how he'd made the decision to buy it, his voice breathless with the joy of giving. He wanted Shandy to love his gift.

He'd worked for the money and had learned about salesmanship in the process.

Justin's chest filled with pride. Their boy was something special.

He carried the coffee mugs to the sofa and passed one to Shandy. "I poured you some orange juice, Josh. It's on the counter."

Shandy leaned in. "He's too excited to get his juice. It can wait."

But could he? The ring box burnt a hole in his pocket as he kept a lid on his nerves. Proposing in front of Josh would be a huge error. What if Shandy needed more time? Maybe she'd want a few months of counselling behind them before making a commitment.

But he was ready—so ready—to kickstart their lives again.

The rest of the gift exchange went by in a blur, while he waffled and argued in his own head about his timing. He wanted to lock this down, to be certain that he'd have Shandy for the rest of his life. He loved her more now than he ever had.

After their Christmas breakfast, he, Shandy, and Josh dressed for a visit to the nursing home. Brenda might not know that they were there or that it was Christmas, but they would remember that this was their first visit as a reunited family. Seeing Brenda regularly was important for Shandy. It was Shandy who would live beyond Brenda.

In the same way that he and his sisters wanted to treat their parents kindly, he came to see that in a way, he was providing for them for *himself.* He'd have to live with the knowledge of how he behaved toward his parents. He wanted to have good memories, to believe that he'd done all he could for them.

How she treated Brenda would stay with Shandy for the rest of her life. If only he'd grasped this three years ago, maybe he'd have been less of a jerk.

Justin held the door of the nursing home open for his wife and son and took her hand as they signed the visitor's log. The nurses' station, festooned with wreaths and tinsel, looked cheery. A decorated tree glowed softly in the corner of the dining room as they walked quietly to his mother-in-law's room. Brenda was the same as usual, although she wore a bright red cardigan over her nightgown. Her hair had been curled and a bit of color added to her cheeks. Her lips looked glossy and shimmered in the harsh light.

Shandy smiled and kissed her forehead. "Hello, Mom. It's Shandy and I've brought Josh and Justin with me." She patted her shoulder. "You remember Justin is here for Christmas, which is today."

"I've visited a few times this month, Brenda. You look very pretty today with a new hairdo and wearing a nice Christmas sweater."

Josh stepped up and took her fingers. "Gram, it's me, Josh. Merry Christmas. I love you."

Justin squeezed his boy's shoulder in support. "We all do," he added.

"My mom and dad are back together, Gram. Dad says they're gonna try real hard to be happy again."

"Oh, Josh," Shandy said in a choked voice. "That's the best thing you could've said. And it's true." She looked at Justin, her eyes tear-filled and intimate.

All his nerves around proposing fled, replaced by joyful anticipation. She was his, heart and soul. And he was hers, the way he'd been since that night at the lake when they'd met.

Chapter Twenty

Shandy closed the front door as a group of carolers moved down the front path to the sidewalk. "Maybe sometime we should join a group," she said to Josh.

"Nah, I can't sing," he replied. "But Dad can."

Justin had his hand on her shoulder and hugged her to his side. His warmth enveloped her, and she looked up at the side of his face. He'd been off today, as if he felt antsy. But as the day was winding down, he seemed to relax. She brushed his jaw with her lips, and he tilted his head to kiss her softly.

"When's dinner ready? I'm hungry," Josh broke in.

"The turkey will be out in ten minutes, so it's time to get in the kitchen and do a few things," she responded. "We'll be eating soon."

She'd planned extra sides for dinner: whipped potatoes with gravy, stuffing with sausage, peas and carrots and candied yams because Justin loved them. She'd used her mother's recipe for apple pie with tart apples. They all loved it.

Josh had chosen the ice cream to go with the pie, but she wasn't sure bubblegum flavor was a complement to the apples in the pie. She'd picked up a carton of French vanilla for herself and Justin.

"Let me whip the potatoes," Justin said. He'd always loved using her large stand mixer.

"Sure thing. You remember how?"

He ran his palm across the top of her machine. "I bought one of these puppies for my own place. I wasn't about to give up homemade cheesecake."

She laughed as she was supposed to. He'd perfected making cheesecake as soon as they'd unpacked the appliance when they first married.

That honeymoon period seemed to be upon them again. A honeymoon without the wedding this time, she mused, wondering if he felt the same way about taking this thing between them to another level. Maybe he wanted to see a counselor for a while before they took the next step.

Justin took the turkey out of the oven to rest while Shandy jumped into action with the last-minute details needed to present one of the best Christmas dinners she'd ever served.

She slid buns into the oven to warm while Josh helped by filling three water glasses and putting them by their place settings. "You'll be clearing the table after dinner, too," she reminded him.

"I know," he said with a grin.

The roar of the stand mixer drowned out conversation for a minute as Justin studiously added milk and butter to the potatoes. Once whipped to perfection, he scooped the whipped potatoes into her grandmother's serving bowl. It didn't match the rest of the fancy china, but she loved it and wouldn't serve Christmas dinner without it.

Memories flooded as she filled a pickle dish from Justin's grandmother. A sense of the women who'd come before her filled her mind. Generations of Christmases shared, and meals served. The laughter of long-ago children and aging loved ones. The smells of the dishes blended into the scent of Christmas and peace came over her.

Joyfully, she watched as Justin carved several slices of turkey and set them on a platter. She poured the gravy into the gravy boat and carried it to the table where Josh already sat watching as the food appeared in front of him. "Wow, this is gonna be great!"

Justin held out her chair for her and she slipped into it gratefully. "Before we say grace, I have something else I want to say," she began as her husband took his seat at the other end of the table. Josh's head swiveled from her to his dad and back again.

She rose, walked to where Justin sat and then she dropped to one knee beside him. "Justin, I love you more now than I did when we chose to marry before. We've aged, we've learned, we've forgiven a lot of things we both did. I'm ready to commit to you all over again. I hope you feel the same."

His eyes had gone wide as he'd listened. Their son seemed spellbound as she fumbled in her apron pocket. She found the foil she was looking for and pulled it out. Her heart filled as she felt the bit of foil between her fingers.

"This isn't gold, but I don't know where your wedding ring is these days. I made this one a few minutes ago." She held up the circlet of aluminum foil she'd fashioned in the kitchen and waited while Justin focused on it. "Will you marry me and be my husband?"

He slammed the heels of his hands against his eyes and then dragged them down his face. "I wanted to ask you the same thing, but I was scared you'd say no or that we should wait or go to counselling first." He looked past her to Josh. "What do you say, Buddy? Will you have me back in your life permanently?"

Josh looked from Shandy to Justin with a wicked grin that filled the room. "Sure, now can we eat? I'm starving!"

Shandy went into Justin's arms and kissed him soundly. "I take that as a yes," she said against his lips, loving the taste of him.

"I'm claiming you, Shandy and there's no going back. We belong together and we have a bright future ahead."

"Our detour taught me how much I love you, Justin Camden, you big oaf." She laughed and slipped the foil ring onto the ring finger of his left hand. "Now, you've claimed me, and I claim you back."

"Forever, my wife, my love."

"Forever."

Epilogue

The Fourth of July – Welcome, WA

As the last marching band filed past them on Main Street, Justin draped his arm across his wife's shoulders and pulled her into his side. Using his other hand, he covered hers where it rested on her flat belly. She'd told him there was a new firmness under her skin. One of the early signs as he recalled. Soon, that small firm area would begin to grow into a bump, and they wouldn't have their secret much longer.

"How are you feeling, Wife?"

"Fine, Husband. Just like every other time you ask." On her far side, stood Josh who'd be the first to learn about his new sibling. They'd decided to wait until delivery day to find out if he'd have a brother or sister. But today, he'd get a surprise in keeping with the level of celebration for the Fourth because if he wasn't told today, he'd want a parade of his own once he learned how their lives would change again come Christmas.

Shandy smiled into his eyes and nodded. "It's time."

"Josh, we have something to share with you."

"Yes?" He craned his neck to watch the last parade car roll past. The mayor waved and he waved back.

Shandy touched his shoulders and turned him to face them directly. "We've got the bigger house now and we thought it would be a good idea to use the extra bedroom. It's just sitting there empty."

"Yeah?" He drew out the word in curiosity. His brow beetled, looking like his mom when she was working out a problem.

"We're giving you a baby brother or sister," Justin told him. "Around Christmas, so I thought you and I could build a cradle and paint the room and put together the crib."

Josh's face went slack as he took in all the information. "Wow! That's amazing!" He cheered and flung himself into Shandy's arms. "Thanks, Mom! I always wanted a kid brother."

"Or sister, I hope."

"Yeah, but I already have Dilly, so..." he trailed off, his face full of excitement and joy.

Justin leaned close to Shandy's ear. "Think he'll always see her as a sister?"

Shandy smiled serenely and turned her face to kiss his cheek. "I guess we have a lifetime to find out."

The End

If you enjoyed *Claiming Shandy* and have ever found a wonderful romance by reading reviews, please pay it forward by sharing a few words about how *Claiming Shandy* made you feel when you closed it. A review doesn't have to be long, or a retelling of the plot, just a few words on how you felt when you finished. Did you sigh at the end? Feel happy?

For more Christmas books, please check out my contributions to the Dickens romance series: *The Tinsel Tango*, *The Rumball Rumba*, and *The Winterland Waltz*.

If you want to hear about exciting new releases and deals you can subscribe to Bonnie's Newsy Bits on my website. Readers can download a free e-book when they subscribe.

Over 40 romance titles are listed on my website at https://www.bonnieedwards.com/.

Don't miss out!

Visit the website below and you can sign up to receive emails whenever Bonnie Edwards publishes a new book. There's no charge and no obligation.

https://books2read.com/r/B-A-JXD-VUPUB

BOOKS 2 READ

Connecting independent readers to independent writers.

Did you love *Claiming Shandy Return to Welcome Book 4*? Then you should read *Christmas to the Max* by Bonnie Edwards!

A stand-alone Return to Welcome Novel: Christmas to the Max brings two charming and romantic series together! Max Whyte (Love at Christmas) moves to Welcome, WA. (Return to Welcome)

Max Whyte moves to Welcome WA to live closer to his daughters after their mother remarries. He wants to fix up an old home, settle into his new position at an IT firm, and try not to think about turning forty alone.

Burned by a single mother in the past, he vows not to get tangled with another woman with children. When he saves the life of a small boy, he finds himself tangled in more ways than he could imagine.

When the boy's mother turns out to be the perfect person to do his renovations, Max has trouble keeping his personal feelings out of their employer/employee relationship.

Kaylin Simpson has returned to Welcome to give her boys the kind of home she wanted as a child. She needs a fresh, stable start and wants to run her own business. Her three-year-old twins keep her hopping, but after she finishes the renovations for Max, she hopes to have her life well in hand.

Max is drawn to Kaylin and her adorable twin boys. Her wit and feisty spirit pull at his heartstrings until he realizes being a stepfather is never what he wanted.

Christmas in Welcome can be a time to heal and move forward and Max and Kaylin must set aside their old hurts to allow love to blossom.

About the Author

Bonnie Edwards has been published by Kensington Books, Harlequin Books, Carina Press, and more.

    With over 40 titles to her credit, her romances have been translated into several languages. Her books are sold worldwide.

    Learn about more exciting releases and get a **free** romance by subscribing to her newsletter, **Bonnie's Newsy Bits** through her website.

    https://www.bonnieedwards.com/

    Cheers and happy reading!

    Bonnie Edwards